"You think them two Hu... ...e. She tossed her head in that di...

"Damned if I know, but if they are, they better be wearing their Sunday best clothes."

"Oh! That's what they'll be buried in, huh?"

"More than likely." He had no special plans for planting them, but he'd like to nail their coffins down and send them directly to hell.

"Who was it they kilt?" She came over, hooked his arm, and stood on her toes for him to kiss her. When he finished, she winked wickedly at him

"A friend of mine, Rip Wright. He was a good family man."

"Was he a good guy?"

"Yes. He was married, had a wife and some young children, plus a ranch. They shot him in the back four times at a crossing on an isolated creek."

"Nice guys, huh?"

He nodded. "They'll be better off dead."

JAKE LOGAN

SLOCUM
AND THE
COW CAMP KILLERS

J

JOVE BOOKS, NEW YORK

THE BERKLEY PUBLISHING GROUP
Published by the Penguin Group
Penguin Group (USA) Inc.
375 Hudson Street, New York, New York 10014, USA
Penguin Group (Canada), 90 Eglinton Avenue East, Suite 700, Toronto, Ontario M4P 2Y3, Canada
(a division of Pearson Penguin Canada Inc.)
Penguin Books Ltd., 80 Strand, London WC2R 0RL, England
Penguin Group Ireland, 25 St. Stephen's Green, Dublin 2, Ireland (a division of Penguin Books Ltd.)
Penguin Group (Australia), 250 Camberwell Road, Camberwell, Victoria 3124, Australia
(a division of Pearson Australia Group Pty. Ltd.)
Penguin Books India Pvt. Ltd., 11 Community Centre, Panchsheel Park, New Delhi—110 017, India
Penguin Group (NZ), 67 Apollo Drive, Rosedale, Auckland 0632, New Zealand
(a division of Pearson New Zealand Ltd.)
Penguin Books (South Africa) (Pty.) Ltd., 24 Sturdee Avenue, Rosebank, Johannesburg 2196,
South Africa

Penguin Books Ltd., Registered Offices: 80 Strand, London WC2R 0RL, England

This is a work of fiction. Names, characters, places, and incidents either are the product of the author's imagination or are used fictitiously, and any resemblance to actual persons, living or dead, business establishments, events, or locales is entirely coincidental.

SLOCUM AND THE COW CAMP KILLERS

A Jove Book / published by arrangement with the author

PRINTING HISTORY
Jove edition / August 2011

ISBN: 978-0-515-14973-9

JOVE®
Jove Books are published by The Berkley Publishing Group,
a division of Penguin Group (USA) Inc.
375 Hudson Street, New York, New York 10014.
JOVE® is a registered trademark of Penguin Group (USA) Inc.
The "J" design is a trademark of Penguin Group (USA) Inc.

PRINTED IN THE UNITED STATES OF AMERICA

10   9   8   7   6   5   4   3   2   1

1

The horse that Slocum bought had lots of white around his eyes. The worn-out cow pony he traded off for him stood hipshot in the corral, his head hanging down, and snorted wearily in the dust. Dried salt on his legs said a lot about his last few days on the trail. "Plumb give out" best described his old horse's condition when Slocum switched the saddle over to this fresh blood bay. The new bronc's left hind foot was tied up on the saddle horn so Slocum's twenty-dollar purchase didn't cow kick him, which he'd tried for the second time during the saddling process.

Ward, the stableman who sold him the wild bay gelding, spit tobacco off to the side in the dust. "He's a handful, they say."

The choice of mounts available at the small crossroads community near the Indian Territory border in north Texas amounted to very little. This four-year-old looked sound, but no doubt he'd be rowdy. "We'll see."

"Ain't my neck he's gonna break," Ward said with a shrug.

"Mine either."

"Never caught your name."

"Never gave it."

"I was just being friendly. Ain't many strangers come through here."

"Two men did yesterday."

Ward agreed with a bob of his head. "They didn't stop for a horse from me either. Bought a couple of shots of whiskey over in the Buffalo Saloon and rode on. I was getting lunch in there when they came in. Hard cases. You looking for them?"

"I'm going to find them. Randle and Ulysses Hudson's their names. They killed a good friend of mine."

"I don't doubt you'll do that." Ward spit again to the side. "They wanted a woman. We've got one here. Her name's Sue. She ain't too long in the tooth, but she ain't no child either. Lives over the saloon. The bartender called for her. Upstairs, she came to the top of the stairs and they looked at her, then shook their heads and rode on. Must have wanted something else, huh? Wanted a younger one."

"I guess."

"Why did you say you were going after them two?"

"They killed a friend of mine down in Dunhill, Texas."

"Aw, I see. They didn't look that damn good to me, not letting Sue turn a trick with 'em."

"Guess they had something better in mind."

"Maybe they knowed too that you're after them."

In the saddle, the three-legged horse wobbled around under him. He checked the horse, then undid the rope off the horn and tossed the tail to the man. "I don't know or care. I'm going to catch them and send them to hell. Shake that rope off of his leg."

"Mister, I believe you're the man that can make this ride. Whoa. Whoa," he spoke to the horse until he finally shook the rope loose off his back hock. Then he stepped away from the anxious horse. "See you, mister."

When Slocum turned the gelding's head around to leave, the horse had a bucking fit. He was going north, making high jumps, and Ward was running alongside, hollering, "Get his head up! Get his head up!"

"Hell," Slocum swore at the man. "If I could do that, I could fly and wouldn't've needed a damn horse. Whoa!"

Slocum and the blood bay went crow hopping through the near-empty street with the bay farting and bucking like a machine. It kinda went together, his bucking and the exhaust. Storekeepers in white aprons were out on their porches with brooms to ward the bucker off their boardwalks and to protect the curious shoppers, as well as their front glass windows. But at last the business was over with Ward and this place. Slocum never got to see Sue, but he figured a one-whore town was something better than a no-horse one. So it was just as well.

The bay finally broke out and ran. That suited Slocum. He was still a day behind the Hudson brothers, and by this time, they'd no doubt crossed the Red River Ferry up by Denison and were in the Indian Territory. Two hours later, he crossed the ferry and entered Indian Territory himself. His new horse, Spook, didn't like the barge any better than he liked his new owner riding him, but Slocum had the bronc snubbed to a wagon axle, so all he could do was kick his heels in the air and squeal.

The wagon owner, spitting tobacco into the tree-snagged Red River, said, "I'd sell that sumbitch in a country minute."

"I would too, but he's all I could find."

The man nodded that he'd heard him.

Later on that day, Slocum bought some grain across the river at a small store, then tied the horse between two post oak trees and got a few hours' sleep in his bedroll. He woke up in the night with Spook having a fit. The moon was out, so he saddled the horse again and loaded his bedroll. The pony bucked some, but they were soon headed north under the stars.

The Indian Territory was full of outlaws, renegades, and cutthroats, so he kept his six-gun handy. The only real law was some deputy marshals out of Judge Parker's court. The Indian police were tribal and took care of Indian affairs, but any crime of an Indian against a white man or white man against an Indian was under Judge Isaac Parker's jurisdiction. Traveling by himself through this land was a good way for Slocum to end up dead if he wasn't alert. He never discovered why the horse had had such a fit during the night—could have been anything, or nothing more than a curious raccoon sniffing around his dry camp.

He trotted Spook, who had another fit or two, but the second fit wasn't as tough as the first round. They headed up the Texas Road—a general term for any pair of ruts that went that way if the traveler was headed south. Texas was over his shoulder. About then a yard dog came charging out in the starlight from a ramshackle dark house, growling and barking at this intruder.

Spook shied into a bushy cedar tree and the stiff branches jabbed Slocum. He managed to recover and put the dog kicker in a lope to escape this pest. A half mile later, the dog dropped out of the chase and went back home, and Spook danced on eggs for another half mile.

The sun came up and Slocum crossed some flat grass country, wondering where he'd find some food. He smelled wood smoke first, then he noticed a woman busy cooking outdoors under the shade beside a two-story unpainted house. There might be a chance he could buy a meal at this place. He rode the bay up close and nodded to her when she came out of the shelter to see who had stopped.

"You looking for a handout?" She was a big woman with breasts the size of watermelons and a large girth around her middle. Armed with a big wooden spoon, she held it on her right hip and kinda slung that hip up like most whores did when they propositioned a possible customer.

"What else do you need?"

"I'd sure pay you for some breakfast."

She threw her shoulders back and shook those big tits under the dress at him. "That's all you be needing, mister?"

"For the time being anyway."

"Bail off that horse and if you ain't got a stiff poker needs fixing, get yourself a plate over there and fill it. I ain't got no milk, 'less you can squeeze it out of me, but there's sugar on the table. I'll bring your mug of coffee when you take a seat at that long table. There'll be a dozen men in here in a short while. Hungry as bears and hornier than billy goats. When them hell-raisers get here, you'll have to wait on yourself. Me and the girl will be too busy entertaining them after that. You've got to make money when you can get it in this cheap country."

He noticed she wore carpet slippers on her feet. With each step she made, it looked like her thick legs and feet hurt her as she brought his coffee over. She put it down and laughed at him. "You want to squeeze a tit and see if there's any milk?"

"Naw. Tell me, did two strangers ride by here yesterday?"

"Yeah. They got here about noontime. What do you want them for?"

"They say where they were going?"

She shook her heavy jowls and shouted, "Katy! Did them cheap bastards that come by here yesterday at noon say where they were going? Come out up there and tell this man all about them. Get out here!"

From under the window shade in the middle upstairs window, he saw a girl of eighteen or so with milky-coffee-colored skin who stuck out her red-haired head and showed him her two pointed pink nipples as she leaned on her elbows on the windowsill. "Who's he?"

"Never said his name. He wants information on them two-bit spenders you treated yesterday."

She nodded and made a sour face. "One had a screw-tail dick like a hawg and the other couldn't keep his up. So cheap, they only paid me two bits each. I'd say that was cheap, huh?"

"Cheap enough," he said.

"You want a fast one before them boys get here? I'm damn sure worth more than two bits. I'll be right up here if you do, mister. The door's unlocked." She lifted her compact breasts from the undersides, flaunting them, and then smiled at him.

"I might do that after I get some fuel in my belly." He considered the notion and nodded at his eyeful of her.

"You won't be sorry." She turned and showed him her shapely small butt at the open window. "You seen it. Come on up, you want something good."

"Best piece of ass in the county," the big woman said. "Even if she is my only girl."

The fried eggs, a little overcooked, and the bacon, really crisp, was fried hog jowls. Her biscuits were good enough and the gravy thick. The coffee a little bitter. He saw why she mentioned no milk; it would have tamed it down some. He paid her the quarter for the meal and looked at the second-story window, considering whether he should or not.

"He wants to see your tits again, darling," she shouted at the unseen girl.

Katy appeared in the window, fondling them. "Come on upstairs. I know you'll like 'em."

The older woman turned back to him. "What're you gonna pay her, cowboy?"

"If she's good as she says she is—a dollar."

She nodded her approval. "I bet you ream her out too."

"Are them guys galloping down the road this way going to bother my horse?" He tossed his head in the direction he heard them coming from.

"Naw, they're punchers for old man Slade. I feed them when they ain't out on roundup. Saves him hiring a full-time cook. And with me and Katy here, them boys don't run off to Fort Smith and get the clap every month."

"Sounds reasonable enough." He stood up, downed the last of his coffee, and walked over to the house, then climbed the raw lumber porch stairs. There was a good breeze and the air was cooler than it would be in late afternoon. Inside, looking up the staircase made of raw lumber, he decided the house wasn't fancy, and the stairs were cupped from the sand-embedded boot soles cutting into the soft pine steps.

Wearing only a pink garter belt, Katy stood in the doorway and grinned at him. "You have a name, or do I give you one?"

He nodded. "Slocum."

A smile spread over her face. "I sure hope that's a handle some shady lady gave you from real experience."

"Well, Katy, you have a head start in undressing over me, so let me get going." He caught her in his arms and planted a big kiss on her mouth. Her hazel eyes flew open in shock.

The scare he gave her took her twenty seconds to get over, and then she returned his kiss. They finally broke free and she gasped out, "Most men don't kiss whores."

"Shock you? Good. I'll try to give you a few more surprises."

"Oh," she said, throwing her arm over his shoulder so her skintight breast poked him in the chest as she walked him across her room.

"Wait," she said and went back to close the door. Then she placed a thick board in the slots that held it shut. "There. Now we can do whatever you want—"

His mouth covered hers and his right hand fondled her breast. It was rock hard, and the half-dollar-size nipple grew sharper under his calloused palm as he rubbed on it.

Outside in the yard, the riders had arrived, making boiling dust, and he saw one run over and hug Katy's momma around her belly from behind. He did some belly rubbing on her butt, and then they all laughed like fools.

He heard her mama tell them, as Katy straddled his leg to pull off his boots and socks, "Katy's got Eve's curse today. So she won't be working this morning."

There was lots of moaning about it, to which the woman said, "Boys, if you're horny enough, there's still me."

He could hardly believe the sounds of the men who called out wanting Momma. Standing before Slocum in her bare feet, Katy removed his vest and put down his suspenders. With a quick step, she moved in close for another kiss and unbuckled his six-gun holster while her eager tongue explored his mouth. He clutched her slender body tighter and made their mouths really work. She let the gun belt down softly on the floor and then hugged him tight. They stood up still kissing. Her shaky fingers undid his fly buttons and his britches fell to his ankles.

He stepped out of them and she raced to undo his shirt, glancing downward the whole time and breathing faster at the sight of his rising sword.

"Oh, my God," she said at last, stroking his erection with both hands. "He's gorgeous. Oh, Slocum, he's as big as a baseball bat. You won't stop kissing me if I taste him, will you?"

"Stop kissing you? Never."

She dropped to her knees, sliding her palms down his chest and the corded muscles of his belly. Then with a moan, she took the cap in her lips and sucked on it with all her might. His first instinct was to stand on his toes to try to escape the wonderful feeling of her lips, tongue, and even the thin edge of her teeth. Her hands gently fondled his balls and he wanted to climb higher as she stroked and slapped the shaft, then sucked on it even harder. If she went on much longer, he might come in her mouth.

Enough of this. He put his hands under her armpits and carried her like a feather to the bed. Once she was on her back, he climbed aboard and began to taste her nipples. Her mouth wide-open, she breathed as hard as a racehorse coming off the track. His finger began to tease her clit, and she moved her butt around to try and escape his tweaking of her large, hard, erect nub. She physically drew him on top of her.

"Oh, put it in me," she cried in a soft voice.

Her legs were wide-open in a V and her butt was raised off the bed—she was ready for his acceptance. He eased his throbbing tool between the lips of her cunt and she tensed under him. There was plenty of juice to lubricate his way through her ring of fire, and he gently pushed himself inside.

"Oh," she wailed softly. "You feel so damn good. Where have you been all my life?"

He bent over and kissed her, and she squeezed his face in

her small hands, all excited. "You're a fucking machine. God, Slocum. I've never had a better one inside of me."

Her ass off the sheet, she returned his efforts as a tornado swirled in his brain. Her stomach muscles were like steel, and the hatchet-assed slip of a girl knew how to please a man. The muscles inside wrenched his skintight dick with spasms of cramplike squeezing. He knew from the tingling in the depth of his testicles what came next and sent off a big charge inside her that made her suck in her breath.

She stretched hard under him, looking sleepy eyed. "You don't have to leave yet, do you?"

"Leaving? Honey, I'm just getting warmed up."

"Good. I like it. Where are you going next?"

"I ain't sure," he whispered in her ear. "Maybe Fort Smith."

"Damn, take me along with you." She wet her lips. "I have all the pussy you'll ever need, and I'll give you some laughs along the way, huh?"

"What would your mom say?"

"I'm eighteen. I can do what I want. She can hire an Indian woman to do what I do."

He pushed his still-hard erection deeper inside her, and she sucked in her breath. "Again?"

With a wink, he laughed. "I told you that, didn't I?"

"I guess I didn't believe you, but I like it." She smiled and raised her butt off the bed to accept his thick root. The face of newfound pleasure soon caught up with him as he increased his speed. In a few minutes, his efforts had her huffing for more air and kicking her legs in the air on both sides of him.

The third time, he finished her off from behind, and she collapsed facedown on the coarse sheet. A smile pasted his lips as he looked down at her. She damn sure had freckles on her ass, and he liked her.

2

When Katy's momma heard the news of her leaving, she cried into her hands, collapsing on a log bench. "Oh, darling, you are so young to be going off. But he'll show you the bright lights. I know when I was your age I'd've given a lot to have been going where you are, rather than staying in that Tennessee shack and waiting for my first husband to come home drunk, screw my ass, and then beat the hell out of me."

She looked crossly at Slocum. "You look out for her. She's wilder than a bitch in heat. But she can't help that—her momma was too after she found that her first husband had drowned in a ditch. About four inches of water in it. He was so damn drunk."

Ready to travel, Katy wore a pair of boy's britches, tight as a drum skin on her small ass, and a boy's shirt with the tails tied at her waist and a few buttons done up. Her nipples about stuck through the material. With her dress and shoes in a pasteboard case, she hugged her mother good-bye. Under the straw hat, she looked the part of a teenage boy, 'cept for her tits.

Slocum rode Spook around in a circle until the horse calmed down some, wondering the whole time how he'd like two riders. He came by and grabbed her arm and swung her up like a feather behind him. Spook bolted and he shouted, "Get your heels out of his damn flank!"

They both stayed on board and she kept hold of the small case between the two of them, laughing halfway to Crow's Crossing, the next spot of civilization in the post oak hills on the Texas Road. Actually they were headed for Fort Smith. He had in mind that the Hudson brothers would head there as it was about the only place to legally buy whiskey, and they had brothels up there as well. Both of those killers had become indelible in his mind when he rode off from Katy's mother's place.

Crow's Crossing had a small general store, a blacksmith shop, and several army wall tents set up in no discernible pattern, so he decided they must be surplus and made homes for the Indian population. Many spotted ponies were either kept in pole corrals or on a long ropes and were grazing.

"How do you feel about riding a paint?" he asked her.

"Oh, I'd love to."

"I'll try to buy one here, if they ain't too high. That looks like the only kind of horses they keep around here."

"Good. I've never had a good horse of my own."

At the store, he asked the white man who ran it, "Who around here has a good riding horse to sell?"

"I have two. One's a mare and one's a stallion."

"I don't want a stallion. What's the mare?"

"Well broke. A black piebald. Smooth mouth, but sound."

"I'll go look." He went outside where Katy waited and saw she was standing by Spook, talking to a tall Indian boy near her age.

"This is Charlie Western," she said, introducing the youth. "We went to school together for a while."

"Slocum's mine." They shook hands. "I need to go look at this piebald mare out back."

"Come on, Charlie," she said, inviting him.

"Is the horse for you?" Charlie asked her.

"Yes. I need something to ride."

They stopped, hearing grunting and a mare's squealing in the corral beyond the post oaks they were walking through. When they got past the bushy trees, they could see the huge phallus of the stallion as he attempted to bury it deep inside the mare's vagina. He was reared up on top of her, hopping around on his hind feet, grunting and hunching to get his probe deeper inside of her.

At last, he gave a great surge into her and she cried out. Two or three more hard hunches into her and he fired a final gun. Limply, he let his huge, pink and black erection slide out of her cunt, dripping all over with milky cum.

Katy laughed. Charlie looked halfway embarrassed, and Slocum shook his head in disgust. "This way we get two for one."

Then they all laughed. Charlie caught her mane and he jumped on her back, pushed her around several different ways, and all she did was toss her head at the flies as she moved the way he directed.

He wrinkled his nose. "She's pretty gentle, Katy."

"What's she worth?" Slocum asked the youth after he checked all four hooves and was satisfied that she would do.

"Five or ten dollars. He'll ask you fifteen 'cause you're a stranger around here."

Katy winked at Slocum. "Bet I can get her cheaper than that."

"I'm buying her as gift for you."

She raised her eyebrows and teased him. "You ain't half as bad as I thought you were."

Then she laughed and the other two did too.

"You know about a saddle I can buy?" Slocum asked the boy.

"Yes, I have a good army saddle, a blanket, and a bridle. I'd take, oh, five dollars for all of it. Good leather."

"Go get it, and if it's good I'll buy it."

"Can I ride the mare over there? It's about two miles away."

"That all right, Katy? She'll be your horse."

"Sure. I've known Charlie for years."

Charlie made a rope bridle on the mare's jaw, leaped on her back, and rode off into the dying sundown with a wave. Slocum turned, put his arm on Katy's shoulder, and headed uphill with her. "Let's go dicker with the owner over the price for the mare."

"I noticed something about you," she said, looking up at him as they walked toward the store. "You make up your mind real damn fast."

"No need in jawing all day. I have better things to do, don't I?"

"Oh, you mean diddle me? Hell, yes." Then she chuckled and looked around, embarrassed. Before he let her step on the porch edge, she feinted driving a fist into his side. "Don't be long in there. I've got big plans for you."

The mare cost nine dollars, plus the man threw in a loaf of bread and some homemade sausage to put on it. That was worth thirty-five cents and would be their supper tonight and breakfast in the morning. He wondered how long Charlie would be gone after the saddle. No matter. They could build a fire and simply wait for him to return while they ate their supper.

Katy had enough wood gathered for the fire before Slocum got back to her and Spook. He gave her a couple of strike-anywhere matches, and in minutes she had a nice blaze going. After he'd unsaddled Spook and hitched him on a rope tied between two spindly oaks, he fed him the last of the grain in a feed bag that he put over his ears. This time the horse didn't try to rear or escape him. Made him feel more satisfied with his purchase; the gelding was getting better broke.

Charlie arrived back as they finished their sandwiches of sliced sausage and sourdough bread. Slocum offered to fix him one when he dismounted his own black horse. Charlie handed Katy the reins and the lead for the mare he'd borrowed, then he agreed to eat one and thanked Slocum. The saddle looked like new in the firelight, and Slocum paid the boy, who acted kinda hesitant about leaving—eating his sandwich slow-like. Slocum knew she was a sweet one to talk to and not bad-looking.

When Charlie finally got ready to leave with his five dollars, he thanked Slocum, nodded to Katy like they had an old understanding, and rode off under the stars.

"You like him?" Slocum asked, massaging her shoulders from behind.

"Great guy, but he has nothing. Lives with his mother and helps her. No future living down here. No work. No money. They own a small place. The ground is not rich. Not the bottomland you need if you want to farm."

She twisted around and offered her lips for him to kiss. He did that and carried her over to the bedroll. Standing on top of it, they undressed and then quickly got under the covers. Flesh to flesh, they flew into lovemaking.

When he guided his tool into her tight shaft, the feeling made him suck in his breath. Damn, she was sweet stuff to plow.

At noon the next day, they crossed the Arkansas on the steam-driven paddle-wheel ferry from the Indian Territory side. Slocum stood beside the bay horse, who acted upset, and held the lead rope in his hands in case he broke. He didn't need him to jump off in the murky, swirling water and drown. The piebald mare switched flies and took the opportunity to rest, standing hipshot.

Hands on her slim hips, Katy squinted at the outline of the taller brick buildings that made up downtown Fort Smith on the high bank they were headed for. She whistled as if impressed and shook her head. "Damn, this is a big place, ain't it?"

"Big enough."

"You think them two Hudson brothers're hiding here?" She tossed her head in that direction.

"Damned if I know, but if they are, they better be wearing their Sunday best clothes."

"Oh! That's what they'll be buried in, huh?"

"More than likely." He had no special plans for planting them, but he'd like to nail their coffins down and send them directly to hell.

"Who was it they kilt?" She came over, hooked his arm, and stood on her toes for him to kiss her. When he finished, she winked wickedly at him.

"A friend of mine, Rip Wright. He was a good family man."

"Was he a good guy?"

"Yes. He was married, had a wife and some young children, plus a ranch. They shot him in the back four times at a crossing on an isolated creek."

"Nice guys, huh?"

He nodded. "They'll be better off dead."

They led their horses off the docked ferry barge. He boosted her onto hers and then he rode through the thick Garrison Avenue traffic ahead of her to find a livery stable for their animals. When the horses were stabled, they went through the mixed traffic of dirt farmers and well-dressed people on the boardwalk.

The desk clerk in the Palace Hotel curled his lip at the sight of Katy, then leaned over as Slocum filled out the register. "No Indian whores are allowed in this hotel. Bring her in the back door and use those stairs."

Slocum put down the pen, grasped a fistful of the young man's shirt, and jerked him off his feet and hard up against the counter. The color drained from the boy's face as Slocum softly explained through his teeth, "That woman is my wife. If you don't want your bag slit open and your leg shoved through it, I want an apology."

"I—I—"

"Apology accepted." He gave the boy a shove and he landed in a heap behind the counter on the floor, gasping for breath. Slocum went back to registering as Mr. and Mrs. John Howard. Then he held his hand out for a key. "I want a street front room."

The clerk climbed to his feet and swallowed hard. With his shirt pulled out and his face beet red, he handed Slocum the key to room 210.

"Front window street view?" Slocum asked, looking at the key in his palm.

"Oh—yes, sir."

Slocum nodded, picked up his war bag, and put his other arm protectively on Katy's shoulder. "If Mrs. Howard needs anything and I'm gone, be certain she gets first-class service."

"Oh, I will," he said, adjusting his tie with another hard swallow.

On the stairs she asked in a soft voice, "Did he call me an Indian whore?"

"Yes. I had to adjust his attitude."

She snickered. "I thought that's what he said. Bet he don't do that again."

"I doubt he's that dumb."

The windows were open and the filmy curtains swayed in the soft wind. Everything looked in place in the room. He put his war bag down in the corner and took off his hat. Fort Smith's heat wasn't half bad in mid-May, but in August the temperature would cook eggs on the boardwalks.

Katy bounced her slender butt on the bed and made the springs squeak. "I haven't ever done it on a bed like this. Don't it get real noisy when you really get to going on these springs?"

"Take off your clothes, we'll find out."

She giggled. "I like you. You can take a hint and run plumb away with it."

Unbuttoning her blouse, she jumped up and wrinkled her slender nose. "Besides, this is my first honeymoon, Mr. Howard. I hope that you're pleased with me."

Shirt off, she pushed her exposed breasts up with a hand under each one. "These ain't simply there for looks either. They like your attention too."

"I'll try to remember that," he said, standing there with his boots and shirt off.

She came over and hugged him. "You don't forget much. I just wanted you to know I love being fondled by you."

"What else do you like about doing it?" He removed his gun belt and re-latched the buckle to hang the rig on the ladder-back chair.

She wrinkled her nose. "I'm thinking."

"What about?"

"This whole situation. You and me."

"Simple enough. Two people looking for all the pleasure they can squeeze out of life." He hugged her naked form against his, and she kissed his chest, reaching between them, fondling his pecker and balls. Then with a sly grin, she dropped to her knees and took his half-full erection in her hot mouth. Working it in and out soon had things well in control, and his reaction to the sensations going up his spine only spurred her to work harder on his dong.

In a short while, he lifted her up and set her on the edge of the bed. She leaned back, spread her slender knees wide apart, then scooted her small ass so it was barely on the edge of the bed for his entry. With gentle care, he pushed his throbbing rod inside her wet gates. She gave a deep sigh when he reached her tight ring and then pulled him down on top of her so he could pump the full length of it inside of her. The thrust of his butt drove his stake in and out of her in sewing-machine-like action.

A tornado swirled around them and soon perspiration greased their muscle-hard bellies as he fought to give her all he had. The tightness of her channel made him gasp for air and work even harder to bring her to a wild climax. They reversed positions. She scrambled up to let him lie on the bed, and she quickly straddled his huge phallus, inserted it, then bounced up and down like a jack-in-the-box on top of him. She slung her teardrop breasts back and forth as she worked on him, and even her face above him looked like a blur. In his intense drive he held back on his explosion inside her until she was leaned over, crying in his ear, "Yes—yes!"

From his balls came a cannon blast that shot a fountain of cum inside her, and she collapsed on top of him. Her hot fluids ran down his scrotum as she gasped for breath.

"Oh, that was wonderful."

The same observation was on the tip of his tongue, and all the time he was wondering if he had another charge that strong left to give to her. He'd have to wait and see.

3

On their way the next morning northwest of Fort Smith, Slocum stopped in the middle of the road to talk with an Indian couple in a wagon going to a powwow. The wrinkle-faced old red man with his large, younger wife beside him on the spring seat answered his question.

"Yes, I saw two white men—riders early this morning on this road. They asked me about buying some whiskey." He shook his head under the sweat-stained, once-gray felt hat with two trailing eagle feathers. "I tell them those gawdamn Parker's deputies, they catch you with whiskey, they will fine you twenty dollars, and if you don't have the money they will take your team of horses and wagon. Yes, it was no use, I bet those two dumb bastards went to Coal Springs to find Marty Stillwater, who sells it."

Slocum looked over at Katy. "You ever been there?"

She nodded and then he thanked the old man.

"You two should come to the powwow tonight. We have big time stomping, huh?"

"I bet we would. But I have to catch those two killers."

With a very understanding nod, the old man clucked to his two unmatched horses. "You two have a good day."

Slocum booted Spook on northward. On her mare, which she called Dreamy, Katy easily kept up with him. He was grateful she rode so well. Fort Smith had proven to be a dead end. No one recalled the pair, nor did he find any leads. A guy he knew from the stage line, which was recently replaced by the Arkansas River Line Railroad out of Little Rock, thought the Hudson brothers had already left for Chouteau up on the Grand River. That was maybe a hundred miles north, but Slocum had a notion his information was good and they had kept a low profile in the river city before hauling their asses out to Chouteau.

"You getting tired of this redheaded girl tagging along?" Katy asked.

"No, I simply need to push harder to find them."

"Oh, I understand that. I hoped I wasn't an anchor. This is some honeymoon for me. I bet I never get another one this neat."

"How long have you been pulling tricks?"

"You mean screwing men?"

He nodded.

"Not long. Maw sent me off to finishing school up at Carthage, Missouri, when I was fourteen for four years. They were real strict up there. I hated the place. I'd always been a tomboy and used to go swimming naked in Hawk Creek with the neighborhood boys. I was skinny, flat-chested and all that, and aside from not having a dick, I don't think they considered me a girl. Besides, they'd've got their asses beat off if they'd even tried anything—every one of them feared my maw.

"I had an affair with a full-blood, and Maw caught me and him doing it and drove him off with a broom. Then she said. 'Girl don't you give it away. Men will pay good money for your ass.'"

She shrugged. "Besides, I liked doing it. Beats washing dishes, scrubbing floors."

"How come she let you go off with me?"

She smiled and winked up at him. "Maw always knows a good deal when she sees one."

"So that boy who sold me your saddle wasn't in on it too?"

"Oh, he might have had his finger in me a time or two, way back. But no, just a few of them cowboys ever had enough money, or if they did, they didn't have enough balls to screw me. I had lots of them liked to sit cross-legged on my bed, look at me naked across from them, and pay me a whole dollar for the experience.

"Maw said there was no rush about me hurrying into the business. I had several good money-making years ahead of me if I played my cards right. She really knows how to do this business. Why, she can reach down, circle their wiener with her finger, and not let them come till she's good and ready. It was all the things she taught me."

"You're looking for a cat house to work in on this trip?"

"Hell no. I'm having the time of my life with you. How far is this Chouteau anyway?" She looked around at the rolling grass country.

"Maybe a three-day ride. That too far?"

She shook her head and with a toss said, "Let's trot. It's not far enough if you're going to leave me stranded up there. But besides, I can stand three more nights in the sack with you." From the mischievous smile on her face, he imagined her skinny freckled ass shining in the sunshine as she swung on a rope out over a swimming hole in some creek before letting go and busting the water.

They stopped for the night at a crossroad store. The owner's Indian wife made them Indian tacos and stuffed them with ground pork. Lots of red pepper in the meat made beads of sweat pop out on Slocum's forehead.

"Can we sleep in his hay loft?" Katy asked, washing her food down with a Mason jar of cool spring water.

Listening to the distant grumbling, Slocum knew a late-evening thunderstorm was building up over the hill. "He says that it's fine, if you'll go up and service him first."

She forced an angry frown on her face. "Huh, you make a deal like that?"

"No, silly, I'm not about to let him touch you. But no candles or lights. He's afraid that we might burn his barn down."

"Good. I wasn't afraid of *him*. It was his Indian wife, brandishing them kitchen knives around fixing our food. You didn't notice?"

"No." He'd noticed the woman had a good, willowy figure and she looked bored to death with her place in life. But he didn't need her. Katy was more than enough for him.

Some distant thunder pealed across the land, threatening rain.

"We better go get inside." She jumped up and went to gathering their things when the wind switched to the north and chilly breath blew on them. Big drops of rain felt cold soaking through his shirt to his shoulders. In minutes, he had all of their stock and stuff inside the barn, with the two big doors closed and latched. The storm shook everything that was loose. Katy pressed herself hard against him as large hail struck the cedar shingle roof like a load of rocks dumped upstairs.

He held her in his arms.

"I sure pray there ain't no tornado out there tonight."

"Fierce storms are usually over fast."

"Yeah, like some of those young cowboys who are in such a hurry to get their tool in me, then puff, they go flat." Her loud laughter over the notion pealed out against the crash of the forces and the pounding streaks of brilliant lightning. "I mean, they go flat right now and hell, you can't get it back up either. 'Cause I've tried."

An hour later it still rained hard with lots of thunder and strikes all around them. They wrapped up in two blankets in the hay mow. Scrambling on her back, she managed to shed her clothing. Naked, she was jacking his dick back to life. When he decided the storm was about to leave, he'd undressed for her. By then she was out of breath, worked up, and ready. He mused how it didn't take much to get her ready either. He moved quickly to plug her gap with his hard erection and worked her rock-hard ass over. Attending to her energy and needs to satisfy her deepest desire was like riding a thrashing fish.

Another wave of rain swept in. Slocum heard something or someone trying to get into the barn, outside the door he had locked in place with a long two-by-four. His finger on her lips stopped her. Raised up, he could hear her breathing hard and feel her body trembling underneath him. But the swearing outside made him toss back the covers and put on his pants.

"Hold up," he shouted. "I'm coming."

Barefoot and with the six-gun in his fist, he climbed down off the loft ladder. He stepped cautiously on the straw-covered floor toward the doorway, ready for anything he might find behind the large wooden doors. Standing by the bar on the double doors in the darkness lighted by a nearby lightning strike, he could hear two men demanding that he open the door at once, punctuated with threats of what they'd do to him if he didn't hurry.

Slocum lifted the bar and the left door swung out, striking one of them and setting off another barrage of cussing. The slosh of the rain and wind made talking impossible. Slocum stepped back with his Colt in his fist. When the next close-by lightning strike's blast of light revealed Slocum, the ready revolver, and his stance, both men threw up their hands.

"Who—who're you?"

"Listen to me. The lady with me does not appreciate your swearing, nor do I. Now get your asses in here and shut up."

The two men looked like half-drowned rats, but they pulled their horses inside to obey him. Slocum stuck the revolver in his waistband and shut the door when the wind swung it back. With the bar in place, he went back up the ladder in the dark to where Katy stood dressed and hugging her arms in the chill.

Again, lightning flashes through the small windows

provided some blinks of light as he heard the men downstairs unsaddling their mounts.

"Ain't no lantern in here?" one of them asked.

Slocum said, "No lamps in here. The owner figures that someone careless might burn his barn down."

"Yeah, well, it would sure help me unsaddle," one grumbled.

"You heard him. The man don't want no fire in here."

"Fuck the man—oh, sorry, ma'am," he said to Katy in the darkness frequently lit by lightning flashes.

"He ain't got no better way to talk," the older man said. "We won't be up cussing long, mister. We're tired from being in the saddle all day."

In the dark loft, Slocum scowled and shook his head at Katy in disgust. Should have left them out in the storm; they were nothing but scum.

Silently, he undressed again, then lay in his bedroll and listened to the drum of the rain on the cedar shingles overhead. None of the leaks dripped on them, and they cuddled in each other's arms. Soon they went to sleep.

Slocum wasn't sure when the cursing one pointed that pistol in his face and jerked Katy screaming out of his bedroll. Then things went black when the attacker struck him hard over the head with his gun barrel several times.

It was still dark out when he recovered enough to hold his aching head and stagger around. Katy's mare and army saddle were gone. His spooky horse was still there, and so was his tack. Where in the hell did they take Katy? Those two sonsabitches were going to pay for this and pay dearly.

He saddled his gelding. Then checked the Winchester in the scabbard. They must not have seen it in the dark or they'd've stolen it too. His head hurt—but having the rifle was a good deal. Where had they taken her? Damn, she was not their piece of tail to take. He had a vision of her snakelike, lithe body and felt the rise behind his fly. Ordinarily he'd have been having a heated session of sex with her at this time in the early morning.

Which way had they gone? The rain had stopped so at least he had muddy tracks to follow—they were headed north.

He went into the store, which had a light on inside, and bought a stick of sausage and a loaf of bread to eat on the road.

"Where's that little mink that you had last night?" the store man asked.

"Those sonsabitches that you sent up to the barn last night hit me over the head and kidnapped her."

The storekeeper looked in disbelief at him and then he laughed. "You mean Bates and Yarby got'cher woman?"

"It ain't funny." Slocum scowled at him.

"I didn't mean nothing, just funning you."

"Who are they and where do they hang out?"

"Up by Claremore."

Slocum narrowed his gaze at the man. "What do they do?"

"Bootleg and rob folks on the road. Parker has a hundred dollar reward on each of 'em."

"What's their given names?"

"Tom Bates, Gunner Yarby."

"They damn sure robbed the wrong one this time."

The store man agreed. "She was a mighty interesting little piece of ass to look at. I'd be mad as hell too if she'd been mine and they took her."

Slocum nodded and started to leave the stupid man. "She was better than that." The dumb bastard had no idea how much more than that she was. Slocum mounted Spook and stuck the sausage and bread in his saddlebags, then took off in the predawn up the muddy road, riding in a lope on the grassy shoulder.

Midday, he stopped a drummer in a van wagon on the rutted way and asked if he'd seen two men and a girl on a spotted horse. The man nodded. He half turned and indicated it was back about two or three miles.

"She looked like she'd been crying. They said she was a crybaby."

"Thanks," Slocum said, and swung Spook on the road. They'd think they were crybabies when he caught them. He pushed his horse harder and knew he was nearing a small town. Since this was Cherokee land, he knew there were no bars, only illegal liquor, but there was always some of that around. More than likely those two had stopped to find some shine. They had no more sense than that. So if they were around this place, they were looking for something to drink.

He circled the small town and thought he saw her piebald behind a chicken coop with some other bay ponies. He turned Spook onto the street and started in that direction. A block away, he found an Indian boy playing with a stick and hoop.

He dismounted and asked the boy if he would watch his horse for him for a while. He took a bill from his pocket, tore the dollar bill in half, and handed the boy half of it.

The wide-eyed boy quickly agreed, and Slocum hitched Spook close to the fence. "You watch him good for me." He waved the other half at him.

With a firm nod, the boy said, "I will be here. So will he."

With his rifle from the scabbard in his hands, he headed around the lot fence and planned to come in from the back side. Closer to Katy's hipshot horse, he stopped in the post oaks and tried to see or hear what they were doing at the shack.

An Indian woman came out of the chicken coop with a jar. She looked both ways and then, concealing it against her body, ran for the house. Someone met her at the back door. A tall, black-headed Indian male looked around, then hustled her inside.

They were celebrating. He could hear them. Someone had a drum in there. Those other two were having fun, no doubt at Katy's expense. He dried his hand on the side of his britches, then re-gripped the rifle and trigger. When he reached their horses, he loosened the cinches so they would fall off if they tried to leave.

He slipped outside to the slab-sided coop wall. The distance was a hundred feet to the back door, and that door opened outward. Not a door to kick in; he knew if it was latched, he'd never get inside. But if he could get it open, he'd get the drop on the yowling dancers in the house. Some were traditional Cherokee and some of the yells came from drunk white men. He could easily sort the two apart.

He was undiscovered in his run to get beside the back door, though there were few windows on this side of the small house. He tried the door and discovered that it was not locked. Ready to charge the room, he swung the door open and fired a shot into the ceiling. The gun smoke fogged the room. A woman's screaming sounded so shrill it hurt his ears.

"Hands up. The house is surrounded by posse men. Come out here or die."

The wide-eyed woman rushed out first, and he shoved her to the ground. The Indian man came next and obeyed Slocum's orders. Then the short kidnapper, coughing hard, spilled out on his knees.

"You don't want to die, get out here."

"Who in fuck are you?" The other, very drunk kidnapper staggered out.

Slocum used the rifle butt on him and he fell on his knees, then went facedown. "Which one are you?" Slocum demanded of the short kidnapper.

"B-Bates." He was shaking.

"Where is she?"

"In-inside. Don't shoot me."

"Get on your belly and don't move. Or I'll send you to hell."

"I will. I will."

Slocum backed inside into the smoke-veiled room. He saw the crying, unclothed Katy tied on top of a bed. She looked like a naked schoolgirl and had been crying. With his jackknife, he cut her binds.

"You all right?" he asked.

She nodded, sitting up, then took the remains of rope off her legs and wrists. "I will be when I get my clothes on."

"I need to watch them."

"Go do that. I'll be all right."

"They have a bounty on them." He headed for the back door.

"Good. I'd put a bounty on them too."

Out the back door, he found both kidnappers seated on the ground. The Indian woman had run away screaming.

"I don't need you," he told the Indian man, whereupon the man jumped up and ran off too.

Katy was dressed in her pants and shirt when she came out, pulling on her boots and looking angry enough to castrate the pair with her bare hands. He found a clothesline to cut and used it to tie the two up.

"What're you going to do with us?" Bates asked.

"Send you to Judge Parker. He'll pay a hundred dollars apiece to get to hang you."

"Huh?"

"You'll see soon enough."

"I'd do worse than that to both of you," Katy added with her eyelids half open.

Slocum hugged her shoulder. "There's a telegraph office at Chouteau. We can wire for one of them marshals to come get them."

"Good."

"Did they hurt you?"

"Yes." But she didn't elaborate, which suited Slocum.

"Here's half a dollar bill. My horse is down the street, and the boy watching him earned this half." He pointed out where Spook was at.

"I'll get him." She took off running.

He tightened the cinches and brought the kidnappers' mounts around with hers. In minutes Katy came riding back on Spook. Unceremoniously, he loaded the prisoners on their own horses, with a loop around each one's neck. Then he tied the end of the rope to the back of Katy's army saddle.

He slapped the rifle in the scabbard and nodded to her. "Take 'em to Chouteau."

He had tied the first one's reins to the piebald's tail and the second one to the other prisoner's horse's tail. They left in a column with Bates grumbling under his breath. Slocum ignored him, riding beside the two in case they tried anything, and he thought about gagging the one to shut his mouth.

They bought a meal from two squaws at a crossroads. It was some kinda stew and tasted good. He had to untie the prisoners so they could eat. The meal was served in tortoise-shells, and the older women told Slocum and Katy they'd make them some fry bread, but the prisoners didn't get any.

The short one said, pointing at Yarby, "He raped me one night at a stomp dance. I'm not giving him a gawdamn thing."

"Did he get you drunk?" Slocum asked.

"It was bad-tasting whiskey too." She shook her head and sneered at Yarby. "I hope your weeny pecker shrivels up when Parker hangs you too."

Her partner giggled enough that her ample belly and large breasts jiggled under her thin dress. She shook a large, dried gourd dipper to threaten them. "No gawdamn fry bread for either of you." Then both women laughed.

The big one shook her head. "We know all these worthless peckerwoods that hang around here. I'm glad you got them."

4

They rode on to Chouteau with their prisoners. Slocum got off at the train depot and went inside to send Judge Parker a wire about where he was, who he had as prisoners, and that he should send a deputy up there to get them, along with his warrants for capturing them. No telling when the federal court warrants could be redeemed, but he would be promised two hundred bucks when the funds were available for those numbered warrants. He could always discount them 25 percent and get some of his money. Fort Smith barbers, bartenders, and others bought them discounted and made good money, waiting when folks needed their dough right then.

When he came outside, Katy was squatted on the weathered wood platform. "They coming after them soon?"

He dropped down and looked across the waving new grass prairie. "We'll get an answer pretty quick, if they want them two bad enough."

"What will we do till then?"

"Lock them up in the city jail. I used to know the town marshal."

She winked at him and said in a soft voice, "And we can diddle till they come?"

"Ain't a bad idea."

"Damn, you're horny, and I love it."

"So do I." In fact, he could hardly wait, simply thinking about doing it with her. Meanwhile, it wasn't so bad, chasing the Hudson brothers across the face of the earth with a tight pussy like hers on hand at all times.

She checked the sun's clock. "We going to put them in jail and go find us something to eat?"

"Let's give them time to answer us."

"Sure, I ain't in a big hurry."

He got up and moved around to sit on the flooring around the corner of the depot in the shade. The two prisoners sat on their hipshot horses looking downfallen and depressed. She joined him, seated on the edge, kicking her legs back and forth like she was on a swing.

A woman in an expensive dress showed up in a buggy. "Has the eleven-ten gotten here yet?"

"No, ma'am. It hasn't come in the past hour." He decided she was in her thirties. But looking at her clothes and matched team, he figured she or her husband had enough money to burn a wet mule carcass on a rainy day.

"My name's Janet Holstein, Mrs., of course."

"That's Katy Howard—Mrs. Howard—and I'm John," Slocum said.

"Good to meet you two. My husband, Alex, is coming back from Kansas City. You must be a lawman?" She indicated the two tied up men on horseback.

"Those two tramps are waiting for word from Fort Smith about when the deputy U.S. marshal is coming up here for them."

"Will Judge Parker hang them?" She looked down her nose at them.

"Fuck, no, he ain't." Yarby said. "We ain't done nothing."

"Shut your filthy mouth or I'll gag you."

"He can't help it. That's how he was raised," Bates said.

"I can help him if he don't stop cussing around women."

"Shut up, Gunner. You've got him mad now."

The operator of the wire service came out with a message for Slocum. In the wind the thin paper blew all over in his hand. "Mr. Howard, here's your answer."

"That was quick," Katy said and bounced to her feet, brushing off her butt. "What's it say?"

> J. HOWARD. DEPUTY WILL BE THERE TOMORROW TO GET THEM. PLEASE HOLD THEM FOR HIM. TRAIN ARRIVES NINE A.M. TOMORROW. HE WILL HAVE WARRANTS. CHIEF MARSHAL TOM HANKS.

"Now what?" Katy asked.

"Get the town law to lock and chain them up."

"Chain them too?"

"Right. I don't trust these small-town jails. Mrs. Holstein, have a nice day."

In the distance, the engine coming from the north made a wailing crossing hoot and was headed for Chouteau. He figured that would be Mrs. Holstein's husband's.

"I trust he'll be on it," the woman said and arranged her skirt with her expensive black leather gloves, no doubt made of doeskin.

Slocum waved good-bye to the Mrs. as his hatchet-assed companion swung onto her horse and they led their prisoners off to jail. The town streets and lots were laid out with weathered wooden stakes, but most of the village lots were empty, save for a few with small houses on them here and there. Two street blocks down on the grassy prairie, Slocum found the wooden jail, and a sleepy-eyed marshal came out.

"Howdy."

"John Howard," he said to the man. "My wife, Katy."

The marshal's jaw sagged at the sight of her and then he smiled. "Nice ta meet'cha, ma'am. My name's Simp."

"I've got two prisoners to hold for the U.S. marshal out of Fort Smith coming tomorrow for them." He handed him the telegram and knew he couldn't read 'cause he held it upside down to act like he could.

"You see that?"

"Yeah."

Slocum took it back. "I'm paying you five dollars to feed them, then be sure the deputy marshal has them, and you hold my warrants until I send for them or come back by for them."

"I kin sure do that fur ya, Howard."

"Good. I'm looking for the Hudson brothers. You know them?"

"Yeah, they was here the other day. After they left I then seen their posters on my desk. I kicked myself in the ass all the rest of the day for not arresting them."

"Chain these two up in the jail. I don't want them escaping."

"No problem, I can do that."

Slocum leaned over. "You can sell their horses and stuff. When I come back you can pay me half."

"You've got a deal. What about her?" He gave Slocum a big knowing grin and a head toss toward Katy.

"She ain't in the deal."

"Shit fire, that would be the icing on the cake of a deal. I'll take care of it all. Bring them kind by more often." He scratched his nuts. "She sure is good-looking."

"We'll see you. Be sure to chain them up."

"Oh, I will. Get your asses off them horses," he said to the pair of prisoners.

Slocum and Katy rode on north. They made camp under a small grove of walnut trees. The sky was clear so he thought they could sleep out in the fresh air.

She wrinkled her nose. "That ole Simp looked like a lot of them bear guys. Bet he's got a dong big as a stud horse and he would smash you to death under him."

Slocum laughed at her impression of the man. "But he's always been honest with me."

"Glad you didn't owe him a favor and he asked for me to repay him." She hugged him. "Why, he'd've given you a fortune to have let him do that. I could see it in his eyes. I'd bet he ain't had a bath since last fall either." She shuddered in Slocum's arms.

"We can take one in the creek tonight."

"Good. Maybe I could get rid of the stink I got off of them last two."

He closed his eyes. "I know I let them in the barn."

"I ain't blaming you. There ain't many coming down this road that are that underhanded. Let's go wash up before we eat."

"No problem."

They bathed in the small stream behind the cover of some brush and afterward he carried her up the bank and laid her down on a blanket as the last rays of daylight dropped into a fiery sundown. When they were dried off by two towels from among his things, they made love and then ate under the stars.

When it was time for bed, she reached over and pumped his tool up again. "One more time, please?"

He laughed and answered her plea.

The next morning she snuggled up to him in the cool air under their blankets. The sun barely lighting the eastern sky, he was back to pile driving her butt into the ground. Afterward they ate the last of their sausage and bread. With their horses saddled, they headed north to look for the Hudson brothers. He was anxious to find them, but all he heard was talk about them being a day or so ahead of them. Hitting the small communities, he found a word or two out about them.

An Indian woman in her early thirties named Hoosie, who fed them their supper at a crossroads, told Slocum the brothers had been by there two days before. One of them rode a gray horse, she said, and Slocum wondered if they were even the men he was after.

"Are you sure that was them?"

"Oh, it was the Hudson brothers all right," she said. "I know them well. They've been up here before. Some whore years ago got mad at Ulysses and about bit his dick off. He has a ring around it from her damage when he gets hard. I saw the mark."

"You saw that, huh?" Slocum asked.

She nodded like that was nothing.

"The other one has a dick like a pig?" Katy asked.

"Yeah." Hoosie grinned big and showed her missing tooth. "You must have had them too."

Katy nodded. "They pay you much?"

She nodded. "A dollar for the both of them, but I don't have much cash business up here."

"You were lucky. I know some they only paid fifty cents to."

Hoosie nodded. "I know them well."

Slocum and Katy kept heading north the next day, and at midday, after getting some information from an old man, they decided that the brothers must have gone west to Vinita. But from there Slocum lost the two brothers' trail. No one had seen them pass through or anything. His pursuit had turned into a dead end.

Jake Austin, a Texan and a big cattleman, ran into Slocum on the streets of Vinita.

"What are you doing up here?" he asked Slocum. He tipped his hat at Katy.

"Looking for a pair that killed a friend of mine down in Texas. They're the Hudson brothers. You know them?"

"I know them lowlifes, but I ain't seen them. I've got a big set of steers up here—over three thousand—grazing on a grass lease. My foreman, Teddy Hart, was killed in a horse wreck last week. I think he was chasing some rustlers. Could you ramrod my outfit till frost?"

"How many men you got working up here?"

"Ten, but I need five more." Austin acted upset.

"Is help available?"

"Yeah, there's always cowboys around up here. Why?"

"I figure as many cattle as you've got up here you'd need two dozen."

Austin shook his head, then indicated Katy. "Put her on the payroll. She looks like she can ride."

The three laughed.

"Will you hire a few more?" Slocum asked.

"Hire what you need when you figure it out. You know men and you know the business. I've got lots of money up here and I sure need to be back in Texas. I've got a new wife at home."

"What have you got for headquarters?"

"It's over on Honeycutt Creek. I'm sending supplies out there tomorrow."

"Who's cooking?"

"Ward O'Hare. You know him?"

"I think so. Is he a good hand?"

"Fair."

That meant he was lazy and piss-poor at cooking. The same one Slocum knew by that name. "I might run his ass off if he ain't any good."

"You might have to cook yourself."

"Trying to keep boys up here ain't easy if you don't have a special cook."

"All right, you can fire him if you don't like his work."

Slocum mused about Austin. He knew the man was too tightfisted, but if he expected to keep his cattle, he needed plenty of cowboys 'cause there weren't any fences, and a good cook was the answer to keeping the cowboys around. He suspected the cook wasn't the best.

"We could go out with the supply wagon and look it over."

"What will it take to get you to say yes?" Austin pushed the gray hat on the back of his head.

"Three hundred a month and enough hands to keep the cattle in control. Plus Katy here gets fifty a month to keep camp or whatever I need for her to do."

"Hired. Let's go over to the bank and I'll set you up with them for payroll and expenses."

5

The entire job of changing the business over took them two hours. They had lunch late. He met Austin's hauler, Walking Bird, in Mary's Café. He was a burly Cherokee who raised his eyebrows at the sight of Katy, then nodded. Slocum had picked up a list of the supplies that Bird was hauling out there the next day from Laremore's store.

"I may get some more things this evening that I'll need, if you can go by and get them before you go out to the camp."

Bird agreed and then he spoke to Katy in Cherokee. Slocum and his new boss found a table and she soon joined them.

"Bird knows my mother," she said, sitting down with them.

Slocum nodded, and they each ordered a lunch plate. Mary's Café looked clean and the waitress experienced. Soon they had coffee and the food followed. Austin complained about several things, but appeared to be in high spirits on account of he was going home to his new bride. At that point, Slocum would have bet Austin's new woman wouldn't match his own current companion.

After the meal, they parted with Austin. Then Slocum

took Katy to a room in the King's Best Hotel and they studied the list of supplies.

She read it out loud and stopped along the way. "More canned tomatoes and peaches are needed, and I don't see any dried apples."

He wrote them down.

"You need some tonic. I'd bet he ain't got any out there. Belly medicine and laudanum, bandages and iodine. More sugar too."

When they finished, she looked over at him. "What are they cooking with?"

"Cow chips, I imagine."

She shook her head in disapproval. "We need a wood supplier. There's surely some Indian who would deliver oak wood out there who needs the money."

"I'll ask Bird?"

She agreed. "He's a good one. I think years ago he would have married my mother, but she'd been free too long to stand being married to a blood."

They used the bed a lot that night and before the sun came up, they were up eating in the café. Bird told them he'd have the storekeeper load the other supplies they wanted, and he gave them an "Indian" set of directions on how to get out there. He also agreed that split wood would be better fuel than cow chips. He'd be back with a load of oak for them when he got back from this trip or he would send a man up there with some.

Bird told Slocum there was a dugout for the foreman and a soddy for the hands to eat in. Most of the hands slept outside unless it rained. Slocum didn't ask him any more about O'Hare. He'd learn soon enough about the man's cooking.

They made it to the cow camp midmorning by pushing their horses. Katy told Slocum it damn sure wasn't close to town and they both laughed. A grubby-whiskered, potbellied man came out of the soddy wearing a filthy stained apron and asked if they'd seen his supplies.

Slocum introduced himself as the new boss and promised

him the supplies were coming but it might be late in the evening.

O'Hare shook his hand and told Slocum he had to get back to his fixing. Slocum could tell already that Katy wasn't pleased with him and almost laughed aloud over her responses. There were three graves on the hill above the sod house. One was fresh and Slocum figured that was the last foreman's gravesite. The other two were recent as well. He'd have to find out who they belonged to.

The dugout wasn't bad. There was an old carpet on the floor and an iron bedstead. Katy took all the bedding outside to air it on some wire clotheslines. The last man's gear was in there, and Slocum found some mail that had been sent to him.

> *Dear Darling Husband Teddy,*
>
> *I've stopped having the plight of Eve each month, so you better think of a new name when you come home late this fall 'cause we're going to have another young-un. Clair, I expect, is going to run off with the Anderson boy, Cliff, just any day. I know you don't like to hear that since she's your oldest. But when a girl that age gets an itch for a man you better cut the strings or you'll have some little bastard crawling around on your living room rug. Then she'll be scarred for life, so I told her to think hard on doing it. Like that would do some good.*
>
> *I sure miss you.*
>
> *Love, Reba*

After he finished reading it aloud, Slocum looked over at Katy.

She smirked. "That woman knows all about it."

"I reckon. The next few days, I'm going to meet the men and figure this situation out. Jake simply wanted to get back to his new wife and their bed real bad. I could tell that."

They both laughed.

"What should I do?"

"Quietly keep an eye on the cooking deal. Figure out what that character needs to do besides take a bath. He can't do that, we'll run him off. All these cowboys have to do is eat and chase cattle. So the eating part has to be good."

"I can do that easy enough. I knew you were uneasy about that part. Jake never did say he was wonderful."

"He damn sure didn't. I took a herd to Abilene once and the damn cowboys played so many tricks on the Chinese cook he quit and walked off. I had to run him down, give him a raise, and make them promise not to pull no more tricks on that bunch.

"He said, 'Good. Cowboys no more play jokes on me. Me no more pissy in soup.'"

"Oh, my God. What did they do?"

"Said no more tricks on him. On another drive, I fired one cook three days out of San Antonio and cooked myself all the way to Fort Worth."

"You get one there?"

"Damn right, and hugged his neck."

"You've had your share."

"Worst one was going to Wyoming with stocker cattle. The cook broke his leg. Got run over by his own wagon when the mules bolted at seeing a buffalo. We all had to help him and he was the fussiest old SOB I ever tried to work for."

"Where will we get a good cook?" she asked.

"We can backtrack and find that last Indian woman, Hoosie, who fed us a meal by the road. I'm sure she'd like to be up here with a pack of horny boys and some good pay."

Katy laughed, "I bet she would."

"All right, let's go have some of his food." He stood up and stretched.

She rushed around the small table and kissed him. "You know we only did it once so far today. You must be rested."

He kissed her harder, then winked at her. "I must be really depriving you."

She narrowed her eyes in a frown. "What in the hell does that mean?"

"Not letting you have all you need."

She hugged his waist. "Yes, that's it."

"We'll get caught up when we get this cow camp in shape."

"Good."

He needed to appraise the horse herd too. Evaluate his crew and learn where the cattle were drifting. And decide how many more hands he needed to hire to hold them on the lease's perimeters. Having Katy with him would make for some good recreation. If the dugout wasn't the place, then they had the whole prairie to use for their bedroom.

The hands were riding in and dismounting, looking weary and then half-shocked at the sight of Katy.

One whistled behind his horse, unsaddling. "She the new boss?"

"Who's she?"

"Damned if I know, but she ain't hard to look at."

"Hell no. But I bet he's the new boss?"

Slocum walked over to where all the unsaddling was taking place. "Gents, my name is Slocum. I'm the new boss." He began shaking hands and registering faces and names.

Tuffy—red mustache. Alex—short and bowlegged. Kelsy—facial scar. Herbert—pock faced. Peter—the kid. Wolf—gray mustache. Shooter—the one with the Mexican straw sombrero. Darby—wore a derby. And Frank—wore glasses. They were looking around for someone called Bronc who had not came in so far.

Blue, the quiet horse wrangler, was an Indian youth. He gathered up the horses and drove them out to the herd.

"That's Katy," Slocum added. "After you wash up and we eat, then we'll sit around and take this operation apart. Since we've got all summer to do this job, you be thinking what we're doing right and the things we're doing wrong."

"Kinda unusual. Bronc ain't come in. I saw him about noontime. He was fine," Frank said.

"He ain't here after supper, we can saddle some horses and go find him," Slocum told them.

"Yeah, we better."

Slocum sent Katy through the line first, and went through himself second. There were frijoles—pretty watery to him—some canned corn, and overcooked biscuits, and that was all. No dessert.

O'Hare and his helper, a mentally handicapped boy called Screwball, dished it out. Slocum wondered what else they ate at their meals. The men shoveled it in without much being said, but it wasn't the most appetizing nor wholesome meal Slocum had ever endured in a camp.

Under her breath, Katy said, "If Maw fed this slop to her cowboys, they'd all whup her ass."

He nodded.

When he finished his plate and walked over to give it to Screwball to dump in the tub of hot water, he asked what they'd have for breakfast.

"Same as always. Oatmeal."

"Thanks," he said.

O'Hare never asked them if they wanted seconds, and he simply dumped the remains off the slope in the grass. One of the cowboys pointed that out to Slocum behind the cook's back and Slocum nodded that he saw him do it. Hellfire, Austin was damn lucky he had this many cowboys still on the payroll.

"What're you going to feed Bronc when he comes in?" Slocum asked O'Hare.

"He knows when we eat around here. He can catch up at breakfast."

"O'Hare, we're gonna make some changes around here. And you better listen."

"Cram it up your ass, you didn't hire me anyway. I work for Austin, not you or that whore you brung up here."

Slocum's fist caught O'Hare under the jaw in a haymaker,

lifted him off his boot soles, and sprawled him out on his back. "Load up and get the hell out of here in five minutes or you'll be pushing up daisies."

"I don't work for you."

"You don't work here either. Now get your things and get out of here or I'm going to plant your ass."

"We'll see about that."

"There ain't no seeing about nothing. Get out of my cow camp."

Every hand was on his feet and watched every move they made. In a few minutes, O'Hare had his war bag loaded and was hiking east for town. The sun was deep in the west and the prairie looked on fire in the orange light.

"Couple of you boys catch up some horses and ride out in the last direction Bronc was seen. He may be hurt or pinned down somewhere. If you don't find him, we'll all go look again in the morning."

"Who's cooking in the morning?" Katy asked.

"Ma'am, I'd sure help you," Pete, the kid, offered.

"Don't leave me out, ma'am," Shooter said, bent over sweeping his boot toes with his sombrero.

"Sounds to me like you have all kinds of help, Katy."

"We'll see how well we can do then." She shook her head. "Darling, anyone could beat that old, stinking billy goat at food preparation."

Four hands rode out in the twilight searching for their compadre. Slocum hoped the man was simply walking in rather than hurt.

"Let's sleep out on the prairie tonight. I ain't much on caves," Katy said. "And if we're going to stay out here, find me a wall tent, huh?"

"I'll give you the money to buy one when you go look for that woman Hoosie on the road tomorrow."

"I'll find her." She swung on his arm. "I bet you want to stay up to see if they find him. By the way, how bad does your hand hurt from hitting that damn guy?"

"It'll be fine."

"Sure. Why, I bet you can't stir pancake mix in the morning with it."

He laughed at her. "We'll see."

The ranch hands came back in an hour. Bronc's horse had stuck a front leg in an animal burrow and broken his leg. The cowboy was fine, but packing his gear on his shoulder had slowed him way down. He appeared to be in good spirits and thanked Slocum for worrying about him.

"And for firing the Irish pig as well."

They all cheered. Someone found a few cold biscuits for Bronc.

"Let's get some sleep," Slocum told them. "The new supplies will be here in the morning and we'll start cooking with oak wood in a couple of days."

He trudged off to where Katy had spread the bedroll, far enough away that the help didn't have to hear their pleasures. When he was undressed and in the bedroll, she scooted her small heinie up against his flank. She reached around and then inserted him inside her.

His calloused hand squeezed her right breast and she sucked in more air. In a second she rolled over on her belly. He was raised up on his knees enough so he didn't crush her and began pouring the fire into her. Then they swapped places and she rode his pole.

"Let me under you," she asked. "I want to really feel you when you come tonight."

They switched and he was back inside of her giving her a race for her money. Her strong legs encircled him and she raised her ass off the blankets to meet his charges. At last he came hard, and she wilted a like flower in 110 degree heat. Sprawled out, she mumbled. "Good . . . night."

He was wondering about the Hudson brothers. He'd get word one day, find them, and even that score for his buddy. Katy rolled over and then inserted him in her. "You want to poke me. . . ."

He wrapped around her and wondered how much more he must do to get this cow camp working. A coyote yapped close by, and he studied the stars on the north sky. There would be lots of nights like this one before they gathered up and shipped his cattle. Damn, they had to cook in the morning. He better get some shut-eye.

The next dawn when Katy wasn't looking, Slocum whipped up her batter with his left hand; the right one hurt like hell. He knew better than to punch a man in the face like that, but when that bastard had called Katy a whore, he couldn't stand it. She may be a nymphomaniac and a wild woman, but he wouldn't put up with anyone calling her a whore.

The hands helped keep the cooking range stoked with dry chips and the heat up. Darby sliced the bacon and sharpened every knife in the kitchen area. Some of the others fried the meat, and when the stack of pancakes reached the sky, they ate and drank Screwball's coffee. Which was good. They gorged themselves till they were full, then ate some more and bragged on Katy's cooking.

She beamed like a possum. Then he told them that she was going to order herself a tent in town and find a nice-looking Indian woman to cook for them who knew how to cook well.

The hands washed the dishes and Slocum saddled Katy's mare, then had the wrangler find her a gentle horse for the Indian woman to ride back. They took an extra saddle out of the supply wagon and saddled him. With his .30-caliber spare six-gun for protection, Katy rode off and promised to be back by dark.

Walking Bird and the supplies arrived, and Slocum and Screwball, the mentally handicapped helper, unloaded it with the teamster. When the teamster had gone back to town, they set into baking some potatoes for supper. There was some butter in the goods, and after washing the potatoes, they rubbed them in butter and rolled them in coarse salt, then put them in a Dutch oven with ashes under and over it to cook all day. He explained to the boy how to keep the heat even all day. He found some sourdough starter and charged it with sugar so he'd have some ready to go after he made bread for supper. There was part of a deer left hanging under some wet canvas to keep it cool. They deboned a lot of it to cook for supper, then cut up several onions to fry with the meat later. For their noon meal, they had some of the venison fried with onion, and the boy grinned. "Gawdamn, that's real food. Guess O'Hare never knew how to make it."

"He knew. He was just damn lazy. And after lunch, you go downstream and take a bath and wash your clothes, 'cause that Indian woman won't let you around her smelling like you ain't wiped your ass in a month."

"Me know bath."

"Good. After you get done eating, go do it."

"It Saturday night?"

"No, it's bath for you night."

"Me do it. My father, he won't come back?"

"Was O'Hare your father?" Damn, he'd never considered that. "Did he say so?" There *was* a resemblance between the two of them, Slocum noted.

"Me don't know." The boy shrugged like the question was too hard.

"Well, we'll take care of you."

"Wash dishes? Take bath?"

"I'll wash 'em. You go bathe and scrub them clothes. Let them dry."

While his bread baked, Slocum visited with Blue, the quiet Indian youth who herded the horses. He learned there were four to five horses per hand. That way they didn't need to feed them grain, using them only a few days out of the week. Only a handful of tender-footed ones needed to be shod, especially up there where there wasn't a rock to be found in a section of land. Blue said he had a few that needed to be culled. Three were wind-broke and couldn't do much cow work before they went to heaving for breath, and two had shin splints, a painful bone condition in their front legs that made them cripple.

He'd need to spend some of Austin's money for more

saddle horses. The boys complained like all cowboys do about there being too much real estate for the cattle to go over for the hands they had to keep them in this district. He intended to ride with some of them when Katy got back and learn more about the range. In the dead foreman's daybook, it showed 3,500 head were delivered in several bunches in late April to the site. But for some bunches he had not made a detailed delivery number, so there was no telling how many steers they had lost or that had disappeared. Most of the cattle he'd seen were doing well, reaching back to lick a circle where it itched, which told him they were really gaining weight. All of them had been re-branded with a Triple A brand on the right, the old brand on them having been vented. Hard to tell about the ears. They had been notched by the previous owners. They ranged from roans to whiteface, a lot less of the old longhorns, but there were some calico colors among them too. Most were two years old, which meant the few younger ones had another summer to build frame. Some had age on them, and Austin probably got them for nothing. Austin knew cattle and was a real hand at bunching them at sale time. But before they did that in late fall, Slocum would need fifty more solid cow ponies and a half dozen more hands.

The crew drifted back in late afternoon and went to sniffing down the aroma of sourdough bread. Soon Slocum got out two loaves of it and a sharp butcher knife, then a pound of some homesteader's wife's butter that she'd probably bartered for food at the store, and he turned them loose. The whole crew sipped fresh, hot coffee and put away his fresh bread.

"Things are damn sure looking up in this outfit, especially when it comes to eating. Hell, even Screwball smells better," the Kid—Pete—said and they all laughed.

They had beans that had cooked all day, flavored with onions, some chili, and lots of fried bacon, plus the bread. They really dug in while he kept an eye out for Katy and the new cook. Sundown came and they still weren't back, but he attributed that to the fact that the Indian woman might have needed to pack her things.

Slocum, Screwball, and two cowboys who had lost the draw the night before were up long before dawn lighting the cow chips to cook over, making pancakes and individual fried fruit pies for the men to carry with them. Things were getting along fine till someone shouted, "Skunk!"

One thing a cowboy hates is skunks in camp. They'd all heard stories about drovers being bitten in their sleep by a rabid skunk and dying in a living hell. For another thing, when they shot the animals, the dead ones usually left the camp smelling bad or had pissed all over their gear or bedding.

Soon a dozen pistol shots went off, and when Slocum went outside in the purple light before the sun came up to see what had happened, the gagging aroma of the damn skunk filled the air.

"How many were there?" he asked.

"Two," someone piped up. "They must have been breeding to smell that bad."

Everyone laughed, but they went around light-footed in case the whole family was there. No one had gotten directly hit by the spray, but the odor was strong in the air.

"Hell, even the pancakes have absorbed the odor," Darby complained, forking in the last of his breakfast at the table, and they all laughed.

"I guess we better throw away these fried fruit pies we made," Slocum said.

"Hell no," came the chorus. "Skunk or no skunk, we can eat 'em."

In a short while, Screwball was washing the dishes. Blue was busy catching horses for the men in the rope corral. Each man in his turn gave Blue the name of the horse he wanted for the day, and he tossed a loop over its head, then handed him the lead. Slocum was planning on going looking for his women since they hadn't come in as promised.

"I'm going to find them females, so supper may be on your own tonight. They should have been back by now."

Several men agreed with him.

"Darby, you will be in charge if I ain't back by dark. You have Screwball boil some frijoles. He can do that. And there's some more sourdough bread."

"We can handle it."

Blue caught Slocum's horse, and Slocum saddled him, then headed east. No sign of the women on the road, though he did pass the wood man and told him they'd unload it in the evening when the hands got back. The plain-faced red man with the hooked nose nodded under his black hat. "I see you then."

No one, when he asked in Vinita on the street, knew anything about a woman who called herself Hoosie. He stopped at the livery and asked the stable hand if he knew her since he looked Indian.

"She was here a few days ago. Then a pretty girl came by a day or so ago looking for her too."

"Where did she go?" Slocum figured that was Katy.

"To look for her."

"Where was that?"

"Over east." He used his hand to wave it that direction. "You ask for King Phillip, she might be out there."

"Thanks," Slocum said and pushed on. What would they be doing at King Phillip's place? Whoever in the hell he was.

Midafternoon, he rode up on a ridge and saw a large number of wagons and tents all around a grove of cottonwoods on a creek. There were lots of horses picketed. Children screaming, running about, and many cooking fires. Must be a stomp being held there.

He asked the first old woman he saw if Hoosie was there.

She nodded and waved him toward the south part of the gathering. He was riding through the camp when he heard Katy calling for him. He reined up, stopped, and turned as she joined him, out of breath. "You get my message?"

"No. Who had it?"

"I told them at the store to tell you we had to get Hoosie's things. That we'd be there tomorrow night."

He dismounted, kissed her, and shook his head. "I never stopped there. I couldn't find out anything. A stable worker said to go to King Phillip's."

"Yeah, this is his party. Hoosie's sister had some of her money and she wanted to collect it before she moved out to the cow camp, because she was afraid she'd never get it otherwise."

"She collect it?"

"No." Katy wrinkled her nose. "Her sister had spent it all on hooch before we got here yesterday evening."

Simple enough, it was as he had suspected before he asked her.

"You hungry?" she asked.

"I could eat."

She swung on his arm. "Hoosie wasn't easy to find. I didn't find her till yesterday afternoon. She had a new friend. There she is now.

"This is Slocum. He thought we were lost."

"Oh, I am so sorry. My sister, who is worthless as shit, she borrowed five dollars from me and told me she would have my money back in two days. But she never came to pay me and I have only a little money from my food sales. Then I found she was out here with our cousin's husband. But she had already spent money on booze with him that she earned as a whore and was supposed to pay to me."

"I understand. Do you have a horse?"

"Two." She held up two fingers.

"Are they here?"

"One is at my house. I was going to pack my things on him."

"Tomorrow we move to the cow camp. We also have an extra one we can load."

"I am so glad to go to work for you." She smiled big. "Cooking on the roadside is not a very dependable business."

He agreed, but felt he might not have a crew or a job left

if he didn't get back to both soon. "I'm glad you're coming to help me."

"Let's go find some food." Katy was tugging on his arm. "You coming, Hoosie?"

"Sure."

He bought them some stew from a·woman Hoosie knew, and they had squaw bread to go with it. Sitting cross-legged on the grass, Katy asked how they were doing at the camp.

"If they all have not quit, I'll be lucky. They're having to cook for themselves."

Both women winced at his words.

He dismissed their concern. "We'll get it all straightened out when we get back, but we need to push to get back out there tomorrow."

They both agreed.

"Oh," Katy said as if she had forgotten to tell him. "There is someone here who says those Hudson brothers are in this area."

"Who says that?"

Katy brushed her arm at Hoosie to get her attention. "Who knew them?"

"Yellow Flower."

"She here?"

"No, she left for Tahlequah."

"She live up here?"

Hoosie shook her head. "She lives wherever the man she lives with lives."

Katy broke up laughing. "That's complicated enough."

"Sometimes I can say things better in Cherokee," Hoosie said to dismiss her speech.

"She say that she'd seen them lately?"

Katy nodded, chewing on her bread. "She was bitching 'cause they made her stay to cook for them and also sleep with them. I think she needed some money and offered to have sex with them for money. They got her to their camp, then made her stay and be their slave."

"Did she say where that was?"

"Were they over on the Grand River?" Katy asked Hoosie.

"I can't recall the place. All she did was swear about the pig-dicked one and what he did to her, huh?"

"I'd guess he was rough on her." Katy agreed.

"The name of that place comes to you, you be sure to tell me."

"We will. Those two killed his friend in Texas," Katy told her. Then she elbowed him. "Did you bring a bedroll?"

"No, I thought I'd find you two sooner."

Katy made a face and got up, brushing her butt off with her hand. "I'll go find us a blanket. Be right back."

Hoosie chuckled. "She missed you last night. She's not going to miss you tonight. She cried and moaned to me a lot—oh, him not here."

Slocum shook his head like he didn't believe her. The notion that the Hudson brothers were still around had set his interest on edge. He'd get them if they stayed around for very long.

At sundown, Slocum and Katy were on a grassy ridge a long ways from the stomp, but he could still hear the drums and *hey-yeah, hey-yeah* in the distance. Hard at making furious love, with him on top pounding away, they became more and more absorbed by the minute, their attention to their sensual peak the goal. In an explosion from the end of his shaft, the head split open, and in pained exertion he came deep inside of her in three rapid blasts. They collapsed sweaty-slick, belly to belly.

Her eyes bleary, she smiled up at him and squeezed his arms. "I'm better," she mumbled and he kissed her.

6

The next morning, he hurried back to the cow camp and left the women to gather Hoosie's things. They promised to be out there by dark. Slocum rode in past noontime, and Darby and Screwball met him.

"You find them?"

"Yeah, you know Indians." He dropped off his tired horse. "Today ain't too damn important to them. They'll be here tonight."

Darby laughed and his helper decided he should too. Then Darby said, "That's an Indian for you. We have a deer that the Kid shot yesterday evening. It ain't too big and we got the ribs cooking, plus the meat we boned off it. That should feed the men tonight. Maybe we can cut out a beef and slaughter it. They're getting fat on this grass and that might be a treat."

Slocum agreed, stripping out his girths to unsaddle his horse. "We'll let the two women take over the cooking in the morning."

Darby took off his bowler and wiped his wet face on his shirtsleeve. "Good, I like cowboying better."

"I don't blame you. Nothing showed up wrong?"

"Yeah, Bronc thought he found some tracks where some rustlers might have hit us. I sent Wolf with him. He's got the most experience of any of us. Figured he could read the tracks better than any of us. So we'll see what he finds."

"That was good. May just be someone crossing the range, but there's thieves all over this country."

Darby nodded, squatting down for the two of them to talk. "Where did you find the women at?"

"I didn't stop at the store, so I didn't know Katy'd left word for me there. But I found them at King Phillip's stomp. Never met him, but I found the women there trying to collect a debt." Slocum shook his head like he couldn't believe it all. "They're getting the Indian woman's things today and will be here by nightfall they promised."

If he didn't know how hot Katy's britches were for him, he'd even doubt that.

"You reckon Austin will sell these cattle and close this operation down in the fall? You know it'll be harder than hell for most of us to find work that late."

"I'll write him and ask. He may have another set of cattle lined up to bring up here."

"I know you can't guarantee us much, but we'd all like to know. Didn't you used to work for the Blair brothers?" Darby asked.

"Yes."

That was in the days of the first drives to Kansas. Slocum recalled those days clearly. Things were tough everywhere, but there wasn't a pot to piss in or window to throw it out in 1866 Texas. Maverick cattle running all over the damn country, and not worth a buck a head down there.

Those cattle were more like deer. Brush hid the longhorns, who only came out to graze at night like feral hogs. Even herded and handled they were haints. A Dutch oven could clang wrong and the damn critters threw up their heads and stampeded en mass for New Mexico or even the gulf. I remember it rained hard in a set of those years, and every damn river was flooding when we needed to cross it. Cow-hands drowned by the hundreds.

There were a passel of small, crude crosses on fresh graves beside those rivers, and they were soon trampled down by another herd. Those men—their mothers and wives never knew where they'd been planted. I remember ole Hank. Why, he could play a Jew's harp like a concert musician. Damn, I sure missed him going the rest of the way up there and coming back. Buried him on a high rise above the Canadian—well, not really. We looked up and down the banks for three days with no luck, and then we drove a cross in the ground up there and prayed that God had found him. We told everyone to say he was buried so they didn't fret about it, but we never did find him or that harp. Then when I got back to Texas, as the boss I had to go by to give his family his pay and tell his widowed mother and the girl who lived with her—his intended woman, who'd held his baby son in her arms the whole time—tell them he was buried in the Indian Territory.

"Yeah, I've been there, Darby. Wasn't no Sunday school picnic either."

Darby agreed.

Darby began his spiel about "going north." "I made three drives up there. Last trip, my cousin was fourteen and he made a hand. But a drunk for no good reason shot that boy down in the streets of Abilene. Two days later, I drowned that no-good bastard in a horse tank with my bare hands. Held that no-good son of a bitch under water till he stopped breathing. They arrested me for murder. I wasn't in jail long. Second night, some Texas boys blew the damn door off the jail with blasting powder. Then they gave me a fresh horse and a wad of money and sent me home. Haven't used my real name since."

"Tough business."

"But damn, Slocum, I ain't a dirt farmer or a store clerk, so what the hell. I ain't rich in many ways, but listening to the meadowlark sing or quail cock *bob-white*. That's really better than anything I know about in this world."

Slocum knew exactly what Darby meant. A good horse, sun on your face, wind at your back—like the old Irish poem asked for—and a man could live contented. Oh, hell, and a woman in his bed every once in a while doesn't hurt either.

Where were Wolf and Bronc? The rest of the men were back for the day and shook Slocum's hand, acting glad he'd returned. He promised them that the womenfolk would be there that evening sometime.

They ate venison, potatoes, and some sweet rice with "bugs" for desert. The day dimmed and he wondered where the two women were. Then he heard horses, and in the bloody last light, he saw two packhorses with a rocking chair strapped on the top of one. They'd made it.

Of course, there were plenty of willing hands to help them unload and set up the first tent by coal oil lanterns for Hoosie. Slocum decided to put his and Katy's up in the morning at a little more distance. It didn't matter. He and she would be under the stars one more night. As they worked setting up things for the new cook, he kept a wary eye out for his two men still out.

Darby, hat in hand, was scratching the thin hair on top of his head. "You, like me, wondering what they run into out there?"

"I have no idea, but they must be like a good hound and staying on a track."

"Wolf knows lots about that stuff."

"I guess so. Come daylight, we'll go look for them. I hope to hell they're all right."

"You never can tell up here. I bet there's more damn wanted men in this part of the country than in the rest of the USA."

They both laughed.

Slocum promised Hoosie that several of them would be up to help her in the morning. She wasn't a bad-looking woman, she had a full figure, but she wasn't simply fat. In fact, he could see several of his bunch had been charmed by her looks already. He'd put her down as sultry looking, brushing her long black hair and standing at the entrance to her tent that first night.

Her salary might be supplemented by the crew's contributions to her fund. He sent everyone off to their bedrolls and listened to the coyotes yap. With Katy swinging on his arm and the two of them headed for their bedding, he still wondered about his two hands not coming in.

More dang coyotes cutting loose out under the stars. He stopped and kissed Katy. That lasted a long while. With her running her palm over his tool, it only added to his being more interested in her skinny heinie. Whew, that woman loved it— but so did he.

7

Dawn wasn't even purpling the eastern horizon when they dressed and were getting ready to help Hoosie. Pulling on her pants, Katy grumbled, "I hope she knows I'm missing my morning treatment from you."

"We'll make it up tonight."

Tying her blouse tail and buttoning some of the buttons so they pushed her small tits together, she shook her head—still lamenting about being deprived. From where they had slept and dressed, he could see a lamp on over in his new cook's tent. Good, she was ready. He flexed his right hand—the soreness was about gone. There was no word about their former cook, and Slocum didn't miss him.

Looking across the wide horizon reminded him that two of his men were still out there in the dark—somewhere. With Katy swinging carefree on his arm, they met Hoosie outside her tent.

"Pretty damn early, no?" she said to Katy.

"Damn cowboys got to beat the sun up or it's a sin."

"I'll get used to it. What will they expect?"

"Why not some pancakes and some fried bacon? They'll like that," Slocum said.

"Fine with me. Let's get some fires started."

Screwball arrived, looking half-awake in the light of the lantern. "I can fill the coffeepots."

"Good. My name is Hoosie."

"Yeah, yeah, mine's Screwball. I-I'm y-your helper."

"He's a hard worker," Slocum said.

"Good. You know, Indians change their names whenever they get ready to change their lives. Maybe I will change yours." She shook her head. "Good help should have a better name than that."

"It won't matter what you call me. I been called lots of things. Some of them pretty bad."

"You fill the pots with water. I can light this fire," she said, already on her knees and scratching matches to ignite her fine cedar kindling. The kindling soon caught and she rose, watching that it didn't go out. Standing at last, she straightened her skirt, then put on an apron that Katy handed her.

Slocum cracked eggs, and Katy sifted flour in a bowl for her. "You may be out of syrup," she told the cook.

"You make it out of water and brown sugar?"

"Yes."

"I can do that."

"We'll let Slocum whip up the batter, and I can put the frying pans on to get them hot," Katy said.

Screwball was already back with water in the big kettles for coffee, and he heaved them up onto the stove. That task completed, he went back on the run with two canvas buckets for more water for them.

"My, that boy works hard," Hoosie said, busy getting her syrup ready. "I will think of a good name for him today."

Soon the coffee water began to boil and the two women began pouring batter into the fry pans, where it bubbled. Hoosie put the ground coffee in both pots along with a little salt. Then they began flipping pancakes.

"Should I ring the bell?" Screwball asked.

Slocum nodded to her and she quickly said, "Yes."

"From now on, that's your decision," he told her.

"Oh, all right. I am the boss of when to get them up, huh?" Hoosie shook her head from side to side with a spatula in her hand like he'd made her a big official of the camp.

The sleepy crew came to the long wash table that Screwball had set up for them with bowls, water, soap, and towels. When they finished and came inside, they peered at the cooks.

"Good morning," echoed across the board.

"Same to you. I hope you are all very hungry," Hoosie said, taking two heaping platters of pancakes to the table.

The crew started in to fill their plates, already bragging on her food.

Katy hung on Slocum's arm. "They will love her, huh?"

"They already do. I need to go and look for the two men who didn't come back last night."

"Can I go?"

"I think you and Hoosie need to spoil my crew with some treats. I'm putting Darby in charge of the men. I'll take one man with me."

"Who is that?" she asked.

"Shooter. He's a little older and tougher than some of them."

She agreed.

He left her at the table area where they prepared food. She and Hoosie were eating pancakes from their plates between refilling cups and putting out more pancakes.

"Boys, I'm going to select Shooter to ride with me to look for Bronc and Wolf. When you get full, come join me by the horses," he told Shooter, who nodded. "Darby is the boss while I'm gone."

Everyone agreed and picked up their tin plates, cups, and silverware to dump in Screwball's big washtub.

Slocum hauled his saddle and pads out to the rope corral. Blue roped his horse, Spook, and handed him the rope. Slocum began saddling him. Spook had settled down after being ridden all over. A long ways from the day Slocum had bought him down in Texas at that livery. He cinched up the girths, dropped the stirrup, and nodded to Shooter, who joined him as he swung on board.

"They were headed south." Shooter said, indicating the direction.

"Surprises me too. The better place to sell any cattle you stole would be up in Kansas."

"If they're tracking them, they may have wound back that way."

Slocum agreed and waved good-bye to Katy. He had some hardtack and jerky in a poke tied on his saddle in case they had to ride farther than they could make in just the one day.

They made good time. Following the land southward, midmorning they found tracks. Slocum and Shooter decided that they belonged to the two missing hands—both horses were barefooted. The steer tracks were older, and shod horses were tracking the cattle hooves. That must mean, Slocum decided, that it had been twenty-four hours since his men had followed the rustlers' trail.

Slocum stood in the stirrups, but there was nothing as far as he could see but rolling grass. They began to short lope. No sign of his men worried him; after this long they should have came back unless they had a hot trail.

A few hours later, they found a crude, thrown-up camp. There were some crossbars on some tall poles that someone had hung beef on. The dried blood and the hides were on the ground close by where some coyotes had dragged them off and tried to chew on them. There was a crude shade where they had probably cut the carcasses up, Shooter decided. No doubt it had had a canvas cover on a pole frame, which they could let down to conceal the wagonloads of meat when they pulled out with them.

"How many wagons did they have?" Slocum asked Shooter.

"Four, I figure. That's what the tracks say."

Slocum was upset about the entire operation and rode in circles around the killing grounds. Then he saw a place where the coyotes had been digging at some freshly turned earth. He called Shooter over, and they used their skinning knives to dig deeper. Neither man spoke until Shooter hit something and gray wool thread came back on his knife's point.

"You thinking what I am?" Shooter asked grimly.

"I was afraid so when we started. This is those boys' grave." The skin on Slocum's cheeks drew tight, and he tried hard to swallow a knot that rose behind his tongue, but it would not go down. In minutes they were clearing the dirt from part of the snow-white complexion of Wolf's face, his eyes that would see no more clogged with dirt.

"Son of a bitch!" Shooter swore, rising up, about to puke, and throwing his large knife on the ground. "I'll kill them damn rustlers with my bare hands." Then he retched.

Slocum stumbled forward on his hands and knees, and he upchucked too. Then the dry heaves took the rest out of him. Sourness ran out of his nose in tails of phlegm, and his eyes soon flooded with burning tears.

"Oh, God. Oh, God. Why did this happen?" Seated on his butt, Shooter stomped his worn-out boot heels, raising dust in protest.

"Someone needs to ride to the cow camp and get help. These boys need a better grave. I'll go find the killers."

"After I get the boys down here, I'm coming after you, Slocum. When I get there, if you ain't got them by then, I'll help you kill 'em." Shooter began bawling.

"Listen—listen! Tell Darby that no matter what he does, keep the cattle on the range. He can hire some help, I'll okay it. But we've got to do that." With his hand on the younger man's shoulder, he shook him. "You hear what I said?"

"Yes, sir. Yes, sir."

"What brand was on those horses our men rode?"

Shooter shook his head. "I can't recall."

"Think, man. Think. It may be all I can hold them on."

"Wolf rode a bay had a diamond on his right shoulder. I can't—why can't I? No, Bronc had a T Bar horse."

"Good, that may hang them."

"Where're you going?"

"To get those bastards." He swung up on Spook.

Shooter swallowed and wavered. "Slocum, I'll get the crew down here, then I'm coming to help you. I swear I want them dead!"

Slocum nodded and set out eastbound. He hoped the man made it back to camp. The thing troubling him the most was where they could be taking that meat. He set his spurs to Spook to go faster; he had some more light left in this day. The deep wagon tracks told him that they were heavily loaded.

In several hours, he found where they turned off and went north toward Kansas. Where were they going with that much meat? No big populace center up there.

Later under the stars, his eyelids became so leaden that he stopped, hobbled Spook, and slept for a few hours. He sure didn't need to stumble into them. By dawn he was in the saddle again and heard a train whistle.

Stopping, he listened. The answer came to him easy. They were feeding a railroad construction crew.

Slocum was in a new place for him; actually he figured it to be a tight spot—the railroad might not back him if he tried to arrest their meat contractor and his men. They had one job to do: build track. Where the beef came from was not their problem, but securing meat for their laborers would be. So he wondered how to handle the matter. This crime was about murder. A more serious crime than rustling.

He dried his hands on the top of his legs and made Spook trot toward the operation he could see. At a distance he reined up to view the scene. Train cars of rails, ties, lots of dust, and a shuttle. Wagons, teams, lots of dust and activity was spread out across the prairie.

No sign of the wagons that delivered the beef. Somewhere around there must be a "tent town" to support this many men. There was no doubt that if he rode east of the rail head, he'd find it. To feel out the situation, he decided that he'd go look at that operation. In order for the highly paid laborers making two dollars a day to stay on the job, there had to be gambling, prostitution, and booze close by. Then they didn't get the yen to leave their jobs and go look for somewhere to spend their money. It all had to be close at hand.

In a short while he rode up the dusty street of the tent city. They were unloading kegs of beer out of wagons—in a dry territory, that made him wonder what dispensation they got for that. Ladies of the night tramped around on the wooden boardwalks in bright, low-cut dresses. Several waved at him and openly invited him to come to some named place or the other where they worked.

One even showed him her tit and then, covering it, said out loud, "I knew you'd like to see it."

He nodded. There was a livery ahead, and he wanted to see if the wagons were parked there. None of the vehicles parked there had been used to haul bloody beef. He could see by the dust on the floorboards that they had not been used lately. He rode Spook around the pens and saw no horses with brands he recognized.

A man came out of the temporary building that severed as the office. "You needing a horse?" the man asked, then spit tobacco in the dust to the side.

"I lost a few."

"Ain't no stolen horses here."

"I haven't seen them."

"I brought all these down from Kansas. Got sale papers on all of 'em."

Slocum shook his head, to dismiss the man's concern. "I don't see any of mine."

"My name's Haught."

"Mine's Howard." He reined up Spook.

"Good to meet you, Howard. What do you do up here?"

"Run some cattle on a lease."

"I've got some good cow horses if you need some."

"I'll keep that in mind. Right now I'd like those two back that were stolen."

Haught agreed.

Slocum thanked him and rode off. He stopped at a saloon with a sign over the entrance on two posts. Wild West Saloon was the name, and he swept inside and studied the temporary bar, which was set up on sawhorses. A red-faced bartender smiled. "What do you need, my friend?"

"A beer. Is it cold?"

"Damn right. Where do you think we are? In some dried-up hick town?" He laughed and drew a brew in a tall stein.

The beer was cold and Slocum nodded his approval. The tent was lighted by wheels of candle lamps strung on cables so they could be pulled up and down. An increasing wind made the canvas roof and the walls snap.

"You need something to eat?" the barman asked.

"What are you serving?"

"Corned beef and cold slaw on fresh rye bread."

Sounded good to him. "How much is it?"

"It and that beer are twenty-five cents."

"Sure." He'd only had some hard jerky to chew on in the past twenty-four hours.

The sandwich that the barkeep delivered in a short while was huge and came with a large dill pickle.

"And what be your business?" The man leaned his elbows on the bar.

"I run cattle on a lease."

"Oh, you are a cowboy, huh?"

"I guess."

"Let me shake your hand. I ain't never met a real cowboy. Me name's Donagee."

"Howard's mine." They shook hands.

"Aye, good to meet you. You looking for work?"

"No, someone stole two of my horses."

"Oh, and that's a bad deal."

"It is." He busied himself eating the thick sandwich. The best part of the whole business. Between bites, he asked, "Who's the beef contractor?"

The man shook his head, then called to another man down the bar polishing glasses. "Who supplies the beef?"

"Rensler is the boss. I don't know what they call the operation. They simply say see Rensler."

Slocum nodded. "I'll find him."

"Where are they at?" Donagee asked his coworker.

"I think east of here they have their headquarters. Some big ranch."

Slocum held up his hand that he heard him.

One thing he knew. What his men had stumbled upon was not some lightning raid by a few drifting would-be felons. No doubt in his mind that the rustlers, like all these deals around the tent town, had an umbilical connection to the railroad contactor. Open beer sales in the Indian Territory meant some higher authority was involved. He suspected, as he considered how to cautiously approach the procurer of beef at the camp, that he'd find that the main railroad buyer might have a stake in this supplier too.

He'd go look for the outfit providing the beef next. He hoped he hadn't drawn any suspicion on himself from the railroad bulls or whoever kept this operation under wraps. These security people eliminated anyone, or even an entire outfit, that blocked or inhibited the rail construction. Every twenty-four hours were precious to such operations. Interest on the cost of building grew each day the rails weren't being used for transport. This made some executives demand that nothing be allowed to halt construction or threaten the deal.

Rather than ask anyone for directions to where the beef operation was located, he drifted along the road beside the tracks until he spotted several wagon tracks leading off to the north. By midday, he could see all the freight wagons parked around a place shaded by cottonwoods by a creek. There were lots of pens, crossbars to hang animals on after they were slaughtered. The strong copper smell of blood and guts intoxicated the huge flock of buzzards that circled lazily, floating high in the air.

Through his field glasses at a distance, he observed the activity going on. Obviously the beef they were slaughtering so openly had been purchased from local sources. The cattle in the pens awaiting slaughter bawled in an upset fashion he expected. The "free beef" they had stolen certainly added to their bottom line. But the operation was so big, how could he ever penetrate it and get to his men's murderers?

He could figure no way of finding the soft belly of these bastards except to slip in and become a part of them. How would he do it?

He backed out slow-like, keeping down after recalling that Shooter had promised he'd track him down. In the draw, he mounted Spook and started back to head off the cowboy. Disappointment made his belly roil and turn sour. Lots to consider in this deal. There had to be a way to get to the murderers, but it looked like an impenetrable deal. He shook his head in grim upset and short loped his horse back toward his camp.

He cut off on the tracks that the thieves came in on. It was late afternoon when he met Shooter on the trail.

"You lose them?"

"No, I ran into a much larger problem."

"Huh?"

"This was no small rustler deal. The beef supplier for the railroad got those beefs. Throwing in 'free beef' goes to the profit of their business. I figure that the railroad contractor has his hand in that pocket. We can't simply ride in there and do something to trip up their track laying without ending up in an unmarked grave."

"Damnit, besides Wolf, Bronc was in that grave too. They'd both been executed. Shot in the back of the head."

"Listen, I am as mad about those murders as you are, Shooter, but we can't simply charge in there. We won't last ten minutes. I know how these big outfits act."

"What can we do?"

"Go back home and tighten up our part—they'll try it again, so when they come, we'll get them on our ground. Trust me, they will try it again. Free cattle are too much of a draw."

"Damnit! I'd like to take 'em now."

"What you and I want won't work. Wait and hold back. They'll be after more of our cattle in a short while. When they do, we'll close the trap on them, and they will all be the ones in a shallow grave."

"I sure hope you're right."

"I am, trust me. We'll have two of our hands stationed on that side of the lease. They move back in on the old place or a fresh one, we'll get them all in the trap and slam the damn door on 'em."

"You see them?"

"I saw their slaughter operation. They're killing cattle at a place over east of the railhead. Cattle like we lost were free. They deliver them to the railroad's kitchen like they came from their place. They won't resist coming back for more. All they had to do was kill two men to get them."

"Slocum, I want to be there on that trap day."

"You can, but we can't act like we know anything or let the cat out of the bag." He still had to wonder when and how many there would be when they came back again.

"I want them sonsabitches so bad my teeth ache." Shooter shook his head like a biting dog.

"We'll have our day. We get a notion they're setting up, we'll be ready to pounce on them."

Shooter nodded, a little calmer but depressed because he couldn't go kill every one of them right then and there.

They rode for the cow camp, not saying much, but Slocum had his mind set. They'd get the killers—it was simply a matter of time. He turned in the saddle and looked eastward. *You'll get what you've got coming.*

8

Long past dark, they arrived in camp on their exhausted horses. The two women were the first to notice their return, and Katy came on the fly, screaming, "Oh, Slocum, I thought you were dead!"

He hugged and kissed her, then he swung her around. With all the shouting and laughter, it brought all the men out of their bedrolls. The girls ran to set up food for them and light some of the lamps in the sod house so Slocum and Shooter could tell them about the pursuit.

When Slocum finished his story, he told them in a soft voice. "Darby, you and Shooter are going to watch for them. Don't make a move against them. We'll go back in force and wipe them off the slate of this earth."

The crew agreed.

He needed to head for Vinita in the morning. He wanted to hire four more hands and buy thirty new horses. At last, after all of them had gone to bed, he finally stood up, tired as all get out, and Katy dragged him to their tent.

Undressed, she pushed him down on the cot she'd set up and began to take off his boots and pants. He could tell by the excitement in her breathing what she wanted to do.

The nicest damn thing he could imagine. In a minute, she pounced on top of him on the cot.

"I don't need no warming up, I need you in me right now. Oh, Slocum, I was so damn worried they'd kilt you too. I have been in such pain—"

His entrance inside her silenced her, and she clung to him and sobbed. He pumped away and she grew wilder with every stroke. Soon her sobbing turned to moaning, and the muscles inside her began to crush his skintight erection. Harder and harder, until he at last exploded, and she half fainted.

"Don't stop. Please don't stop, I'll catch you, I—will."

Later, they fell from their passion into a deep sleep, still in each other's arms. In the predawn, Hoosie's hissing woke them. He told her that they were coming. His eyes felt like sandpits as he sat on the edge of the bed pulling on his socks. Vinita came next. After breakfast and the crew had gone, he kissed Katy good-bye and headed for town.

He went by the mercantile with the list of supplies the women had made for Walking Bird to bring out, plus another wood order too. Things were going well, and while he sipped on a warm beer in the Lion's Bar, he asked the bartender if there were any unemployed hands around worth hiring.

"A few. Where are you at?"

"The Triple A outfit, out beyond Honeycutt Creek."

"I'll send you some if I think they'll work."

"Two bucks a head for who I hire."

"You've got a deal."

"Where's this railroad I hear about headed?"

"Comes out of Missouri and heading for Enid. Missed us—we'd like to have been the cross tracks here."

Slocum nodded. "There will be tracks all over someday."

"Yeah, they say they're really building that one."

Slocum finished his beer and nodded. "Anyone around here ever work for them?"

"What did you need to know?"

"I'm missing a few horses. They may have wandered off in that direction, I simply wondered about them. Maybe they'd seen them."

The barkeep leaned over the bar to whisper, "They told me even Parker's men are not allowed up there." He looked around to be certain no one could hear him. "They run that deal with a steel fist."

"Most of those big outfits do."

"They've got connections clear back to D.C."

"How do you sell beer here?"

"It's only 2.2. You won't get drunk on it. We don't have any whiskey or wine either."

"I see." Slocum smiled and agreed, learning something else.

"I'll send you some help."

"Good deal." He wondered if that was all that they were serving in the railroad camp, but he doubted it. "Thanks."

Slocum spoke to the liveryman, Hank, about needing men, and Hank called up two young men who were pitching manure out of the barn into a wagon.

"This guy runs the Triple A cow camp on Honeycutt Creek. Either of you want to go to work for him?"

The two looked pretty shabby. Hadn't shaved or had a haircut in a while. Both were in their late teens.

"Is it shoveling shit?" the tall one asked.

"No, it's riding a horse all day, keeping those cattle on the lease land."

"I ain't got a horse."

"No problem. I've got horses. Walking Bird can haul you two out there tomorrow when he brings our supplies."

"My name's Dean. This here's my cousin Kent." They pulled off their tattered gloves to shake his hand.

"If you guys are coming, I'll advance you two dollars to clean up. Shave, get a haircut, and wash those clothes. Don't buy no beer. Bring a bedroll, a slicker, and a saddle with a bridle."

"We can do that." Dean spoke to Hank. "Hate to leave you, sir. But real work calls."

The liveryman laughed. "I'll still have shit to load when you two come back."

Both nodded and thanked him. Slocum gave them the money.

"They're good workers," Hank promised him.

Slocum also gave the man fifty cents to buy him some weak beer and mounted Spook to ride home. He had two more men, and that should help, and the bartender promised to send him more.

His big concern was when the *butchers* would be coming back. That could be sooner or later. He hoped he was ready for them. No way he wanted to lose any more hands to them. The notion made his belly roil.

Back in camp, he discovered they'd saved him some supper. He ate after dark with a lamp and the two women for company. Slocum and Katy parted with Hoosie and told her to get them up to help in the morning.

So when they came in the dark the next morning before she even had a chance to wake them up, Hoosie met them, ready to get working.

"I renamed Screwball today," Hoosie said. "His new name is Buddy. That boy is good, and he really works hard."

Busy building a fire in her range, she stopped talking when her helper came in and said, "Hi, everyone. I'll go get the coffee water."

"Morning, Buddy. Good, you go get it."

"Morning to each of you." And he was gone to fetch the water.

"I don't know much about his origin. Buddy said the ex-cook was his father."

"He did tell us that," Katy added, "but he says he don't know much about it."

"His mind can't take much on at one time." Slocum was

grinding the roasted coffee beans. "Or he goes into being confused."

Hoosie agreed, busy slicing potatoes while Katy made the biscuit dough. The operation was well under way.

"I hired two more young cowboys in town. They were cleaning out a livery barn there. I don't know if they can even sit a horse."

They laughed. Buddy was back and put the gallon-size pots on the stove. "I'll fill my wash tubs next."

"You're doing good," Hoosie said and laughed.

He stopped in the doorway. "I like to hear you laugh. It makes me want to laugh too."

"Well, laugh away, Buddy. We've got lots to do."

"I will. I promise."

"See what she means." Katy said under her breath.

"I'm glad he's working out. You need his strength." Slocum finished the coffee grinding. Next, he greased the Dutch oven and set the cast-iron pot on a pile of hot ashes. Katy brought him the ready-to-bake biscuits, and he started loading it with them. That done, he put on the lid and covered it in hot ashes. She went to make more biscuits, and he greased the second Dutch oven.

The potatoes sizzled in the frying pans and Hoosie started grease and flour in the third one to make gravy. They were rolling along. The second set of biscuits were placed in the Dutch oven, then Slocum checked on the first set and whirled the top around to reset the upper heat. Then he went and helped Katy open some cans of peaches to set out on the table for the men.

"You really spoil these guys," Katy teased him.

"I'd rather have spoiled help than griping ones. They work harder that way."

"It does work." Katy winked at him.

Hoosie added the ground coffee to the two pots and sighed. "Why, I'd have to get up an hour earlier if I didn't have Katy and Buddy and you, boss man."

She hugged his neck and kissed him on the cheek as he sat on the bench opening cans. "You are something else. This is the best job I've ever had in my life."

"Good." He was glad to have that team.

"Buddy, it's time to ring the bell," Hoosie said.

"I'll do it."

With his hand wrapped in his kerchief, Slocum took a tin cup of hot coffee and went out on the porch as the sleepy-headed crew staggered up to wash their hands and faces.

A round of "Morning, boss" sounded like a choir.

"Good day, gents."

"You learn anything in town?" Shooter asked.

"Nothing worth a dime."

"We're watching for 'em."

"Trust me. They'll come back. Greed is a powerful thing."

"I hear you," Shooter said and went off to take his place.

"Walking Bird coming today?" Frank asked, busy cleaning his eyeglasses.

"Sure, what do you need?" Slocum asked.

"Oh, I'm expecting a letter."

"You never write no letters," someone quipped and then followed it up with a question. "Who'd write you?

"My wife."

"You got a wife?" the Kid asked.

"Sure, and she's supposed to have a baby about now."

"Where is she at?" Slocum asked.

"Arkansas. She lives on her folks' farm."

"I could pay you and you could run home for a few days when I get more help in here," Slocum offered.

He hooked his glasses up and nodded. "I'd sure appreciate that."

"Remind me."

"Oh, I will."

Slocum nodded. "I hear Blue and the horses coming in. Tell him to cut out Spook for me."

"We'll do it," someone said as the men all dashed down their coffees and finished the last bits of peaches on their plates. All the sugary juice in the cans was gone. Slocum wanted to laugh. They were quite a crew. The missing two men were as good as any cowboys who'd ever straddled a horse. He owed them plenty. Shame they hadn't ridden back for help. No one would ever know what had really happened to them. Outnumbered was what Slocum figured.

He needed to spend a day working on the books. Who he'd hired, who he owed what to. How much of Austin's money he'd spent. The cattle all looked great. They were putting on the weight on that good grass, which was the entire purpose of the project. Some rain would help, but he couldn't help that. It had clouded up several evenings, then blown itself out.

"Someone's coming," Katy said, sticking her head inside the door. The two women had been busy making apple pies.

"Do I know them?"

"They're coming from the north."

He snuffed. "Hmm." Then thanked her and rose to go meet them. There were three men in brown suits, headed for the cow camp. What did they want? Maybe they were Parker's men. They were all dressed up.

The rider in the middle looked to be in charge: a big man with hard eyes who surveyed things, then dismounted and handed the one on the right his reins.

"This your headquarters?" the man asked, still inspecting.

"It's Jake Austin's. I'm the manager."

"Where's Austin?"

"In San Antonio, Texas. What do you need?"

"Ralph Rensler, the Great Western Provision Company."

"Slocum's my name." They shook hands.

"I'm looking for beef to buy. We provide the Kansas City Iron and Steel Corporation with beef and food. What would you sell me some good beef for, that we'd take up to my slaughter operation northeast of here?"

"I imagine fifteen cents a pound on some good scales."

"You do work for the man." Rensler shook his head as if amazed he'd even ask that much. "I'm buying fat cattle every day for six cents up here."

"Better not quit buying from them."

"I might pay seven if they were real good."

"That won't buy these." Slocum already had the notion that the pair on horseback were Rensler's enforcers. Twice Rensler had thrown his hand up for them to stay out of it. The message was clear enough: Sell or get the hell beat out of you. He had no wish to be in a gunfight against three of them, but they'd do to watch.

"How do I contact this Jake Austin? He might have other ideas about this falling beef market, since you are so remote from reality."

"Wire him at the Stockyards in San Antonio. He has an office there."

"Fine, I'll do that. Don't be surprised if you get orders to sell. He's in the business and knows how tough times are right now."

"We'll see."

Rensler was about to remount. "Tell those three employees of yours with those shotguns that I saw them and I don't appreciate having a gun pointed at me."

"They feel that if they or anyone here is being threatened, they should shoot first and ask questions later."

"You know what you need?" he said, mounting and then sharply checking his horse.

"I'm listening."

"A good lesson in manners."

Slocum's eyelids were set in slits, and he drew in deep breaths through his nose. "Anytime you want to come and fight, just say so. We'll see who does what. Now clear the hell out of here."

"You haven't heard the last of me." They galloped off with his last man twisted in the saddle, keeping his eyes on Slocum like he expected to be shot in the back.

Katy rushed out and hugged him. "I'm glad that you're all right. Those men are mean."

"Not half as mean as I'll be when they try to raid us again."

"That was one of them?" She looked aghast.

"He's the one that runs that whole outfit."

"No wonder you were so pissed."

"What will we do—I mean if they come back here?" Hoosie asked.

"Shoot 'em."

"I guess we can do that." Katy looked hard at Hoosie, who nodded.

"Think hard. It's their lives or yours that will be at stake," Slocum said.

Katy shook her head. "I'll be glad when this is all over."

He hugged her shoulder. "So will I."

That evening, Shooter and Darby came in late. The crew was already eating. Slocum took his coffee and went to meet them.

"What's happening?" he asked, squatting on his boot heels.

"There were four rustlers today. We discovered them moving some cattle easy to the south toward that slaughter site. They didn't see us." Darby said.

"Their boss and two henchmen were here earlier, wanting to buy them for six cents a pound. I figure they were testing us and then bitched when Katy, Hoosie, and Buddy covered them with shotguns."

Shooter laughed. "Good for you girls. Wished you'd shot their damn asses off."

"He conveniently rode in here to test the water is all," Slocum said.

"What do we do next?" Darby asked.

"If they're gathering another kill, we need to be ready to ride down there and confront them. They choose to fight, we'll answer them with bullets."

"Last time they were in and out at lightning speed." Shooter said.

"We'll be watching them this time. I'll talk to the crew tonight."

Both men agreed.

While his last two hands ate, he told the rest what was

about to happen. "If anyone here is afraid or doesn't want to ride down there, he can stay here and guard the camp."

No one answered his call. He nodded and went on. "Now, the two men they killed must have ridden in, and the rustlers got the drop on them. Then they were executed. Remember, these are killers. Cover your backside. We'll ride down that way about 3 A.M. Blue, keep the horses ready. You women will need to have coffee ready and something to eat. It'll be a long day."

He paused. "Any questions?"

"Whew," one cowboy said, filing out with the rest. "Sounds like a tough picnic."

It might be. But it was them or his outfit, Slocum decided, sipping on a fresh cup of coffee.

Everyone turned in early. The seriousness of the pending deal made Slocum and Katy hold each other under the blanket until they fell asleep. Two A.M. came quickly, and Hoosie woke them to help her. Slocum was so absorbed in what he needed to do to lead his men that he was hardly present with them. All the ins and outs of the coming confrontation. What to expect. He didn't need a train wreck to happen to his bunch either.

After the meal, the men got up and caught their horses, saddled, and rode out. Slocum had handed out five rifles to the best shooters, along with plenty of ammo, and the rest had six-guns. Some had two. The ride was two hours long and Slocum could see that the lights were on at the killing camp. That was how they did the butchering: They strung coal oil lamps on the same poles the beef hung on. A flurry of activity was going on. His crew hid their horses in a draw at a good distance and hobbled them. Then he gave Darby half of the men to come in from the northwest; his bunch would sneak in from the northeast. They left their chaps and spurs on their saddles.

Slocum saw no armed guards on horseback, but he told them all to watch for some. They ran low and only so far, then they dropped to their knees. There was enough starlight, but no moon. They had planned it that way. Still, no clouds and just stars were enough for him and his men with the rustlers' lighting to guide them.

Slocum could hear the rustlers' cussing. They were close enough. He rose and cupped his hands. "Hands in the air. Anyone goes for a gun will die—"

A shot went off from Darby's side, and one of the rustlers who'd pulled a handgun was knocked over on his back.

"Anyone else want to die?"

No answer. Most of the rustlers held their hands up as Slocum's crew hurried in to take charge of nearly two dozen men. Slocum spotted a man crouched on his knees behind a skinned carcass, preparing to come up shooting. Slocum paused and took aim down the sights of the .44/40 Winchester. Then he fired.

Hit in the face, the man flew backward. His pistol went off in the sky. The crew wasted no time moving in and disarming the rest of them. The butchering crew was soon seated on the ground with their hands tied behind their backs. Three of Slocum's men were on guard, and the rest were searching the prairie for any sign of opposition.

"Who's in charge here?" Slocum asked.

"You're going to regret this, mister," spoke up one man. "You don't know who you're messing with."

"Sorry, but I do. The Great Western Provision Company. A Mr. Rensler. Met him yesterday.

"We're not going to mess with you long. You'll be in Fort Smith in Judge Parker's courtroom. He hates killers and rustlers. You killed two of our men."

"You won't ever get us there."

"That'll be your choice because if you think we're going to turn you loose, you all are dreaming. We're going to gun all of you down if you make one move."

"You don't have any authority—"

"You better shut up or I'll gag you. Darby, check the wagons. They're all tied up. I want a fresh hide with a Triple A brand on it as evidence. We'll need two wagons to haul these men in. We'll take the rest of the teams and saddle horses with us. We'll burn the balance of the wagons."

"Yes, sir. Shooter, take two men and get our saddle horses up here."

"I've got them."

"Good," Slocum said. "I want to be on the road to Vinita as quick as we can."

"Listen," one of the outlaws shouted. "Whoever you are, you better turn us loose or you won't ever live through this."

Same mouthy leader. Slocum went over to the wagon where the man sat on his butt in the wagon bed. "What's your name?"

"Pauly."

"Pauly, you better save your breath, for the last one you'll take will be on that scaffold beside the Arkansas River. Gag him. I'm tired of hearing him."

"I've got him," one of his men said. In seconds the leader was gagged with his own neckerchief.

With one of his cowboys on each spring seat to drive the teams, the extra teams still in harness as well as several saddled horses were driven in a bunch. The Kid took charge of herding the loose ones. Slocum left Darby and two others to burn the remaining wagons. The outfit would damn sure be short on conveyances after this.

They left in a trot headed east. The sun was about to light the sky.

"They may send someone to check on them or guard their return. Be ready for anything," Slocum told his men, riding up and down the line of wagons and horses. Smoke streaked the sky over his shoulder. Darby and the other two would soon catch up. Destroying those wagons meant fewer wagons for the rustlers' operation to haul off their ill-gotten meat next time. The cowboys rode in a long trot as the sun heated the day. Shooter scouted ahead and soon came riding back.

"I counted five riders headed this way," Shooter said with a frown.

Slocum held up his arm to halt the men. "Put the wagons in a V up there on that rise so they'll have to shoot their own men to get to us. When all hell breaks loose, we have to be certain that none escape to go back for help."

The five men came closer and then stopped within easy rifle range. Each of Slocum's men who had a rifle rested his barrel on a wagon box and had targets that Darby had chosen for them.

"Halt," the man on the dun horse shouted.

"Throw your guns down," Slocum ordered. "If you shoot, you will kill your own men, who I have in these wagons. Get Pauly up, so they can see him."

The driver, Kelsey, jumped over in back, forced Pauly to his feet, and took off the gag. "Tell them."

"Hold your fire. He's got all of us in here," Pauly shouted.

One of the riders aimed a rifle at them. He never got to squeeze the trigger. The barrage of gunshots from the wagons leveled the field, save for one rider, and he jerked his horse around to escape.

"I'll get him," Slocum said and put the spurs to Spook.

The rider discarded his rifle and swept back his coat to try to get to his pistol, not watching where his horse was headed and fighting the pistol that he drew. The sight hung on his flapping coat. His horse darted left, shying from something that the animal saw or imagined. The rider spilled off onto the ground. He rolled over and tried to fire his handgun at Slocum—too late, too shaky a shot. Slocum's second bullet struck him in the chest. Slocum never stopped—catching the horse was his next task. He didn't need the beast to run home and let them know something was wrong.

His Colt jammed in his holster, he shook out a rope and began to build a loop. He pressed Spook harder and closed in on the runaway. When the loop passed over the horse's ears, Slocum set on the brakes, and Spook set down. He reached down, caught the runaway horse's reins, and led him back.

The crew had all the other horses caught. The dying man

and the other two wounded ones were tied and then tossed in the wagon. The two dead ones were draped over their horses and tied down. Their operation was on the move again.

"You figure they can stop us?" Darby asked.

"No. But they're tough." Slocum shook his head. Speed was of the essence so that the big boys didn't learn soon enough how to squelch his plans. Once he got these prisoners to Fort Smith, their lawyers could argue with the wind better than they could with Judge Parker.

"How are we getting them to Fort Smith?"

"I'll let the marshals figure that out. There's an office in Vinita."

"When will we get there?"

"Midafternoon or so, I figure."

"So we can hope Rensler has no idea that we've done this?" Darby asked.

Slocum nodded. "So far anyway."

"I knew that's why you'd taken their horses."

With a nod, Slocum forced a smile. "We need to do all we can to get them into that hellhole under the courthouse."

"Amen."

At noontime they stopped and put fresh teams on the wagons. Anyone with a spent horse took one of the extras from the rustlers' camp. The stop was short. Everyone and all the stock got a drink, except for the outlaws. Then they were going again eastbound.

Past the road to the railhead, Slocum eased up some. He must have enough of Rensler's slaughter crew, not to mention five of his guards, that the man must be wondering where in the hell they were all at. But Rensler would need to either read tracks or go back to the killing site and follow Slocum's group from there. He prayed for them to have to go back to the start. No telling.

By midafternoon, after pushing hard, all their horses had nearly given out. Slocum began to worry, and they took a short thirty-minute break at another watering hole. His men used a bucket, giving the rustlers a drink from the lip of the pail.

"I got to piss," one complained.

"Well, piss in your pants. I ain't getting it out for you." Frank said, moving on to water the next one.

At six o'clock, according to the clock on the wall of the U.S. marshal's office in Vinita, they arrived. The young clerk jumped at Slocum's entry.

"I have more than twenty rustlers and killers outside that we need to ship to Fort Smith tonight."

"Who? Who are you sir?"

"Who is your boss?"

"Under Marshal Ely Hindman."

"Is he in town?"

"At home. "

"You go find him right now. These prisoners have a posse coming to rescue them. We'll watch the jail."

"This is highly irregular, sir. Oh, I will. Your name?"

"Slocum."

The young man grabbed his hat and tore out of the office.

Darby had stepped back to let him fly past.

"How are we?" Slocum asked.

Darby nodded. "The extra horses and teams are at the livery. We left the wagons hitched up."

"Good."

So close. If their luck held, it would be because Rensler was so confident that he could do anything he demanded that he didn't worry too much about his men being caught. Enough said. Slocum paced the office floor until a hatless older man burst in.

"What's going on here? I'm Marshal Ely Hindman. Looks to me like you and your men are ready for war. Who are those men in the wagons?"

"If this was not dead serious, I would not be here, sir." Slocum began to tell the lawman the facts, starting with the execution of his two cowboys. He finished with, "We set the trap and caught them. Five armed men tried to stop us. Three are dead, two arc wounded."

Looking impressed, Hindman shook his head. "You've cut down some tall timber."

"What will you do?"

"I'll have the railroad hook a freight car on the back of a passenger train and haul them to Muskogee in a few hours. Then have marshals waiting to take them to Fort Smith by wagon from there. That will be the quickest way and the hardest to interrupt. My clerk is en route and can take down depositions from them, and they will be incarcerated until the grand jury can meet. Parker won't allow any bonds in a case like this for any of them."

"There will be some angry, highly paid lawyers demanding their release."

"Federal Judge Isaac Parker is not influenced by such men."

"Good. I need to get back to my camp. Should I send along the two men who scouted their rustling and dug up the dead men to testify?"

"That would not be a bad idea."

"I'll send them and get back to the camp before the rest of the stock disappears. I have several head of horses that they used in this operation. How can you hold them?"

"I'll slap a federal evidence hold on them, and they can't be moved."

"Good." Rensler would have to replace them. Slocum wanted to smile. "You and your men can hold and load them on the train."

"Yes. I have more help coming."

Slocum stopped and turned back. "Sounds good. Is it legal to sell 2.2 beer in the territory?"

"Hell no, sir. Where are they doing that?"

"In the saloon in town."

Hindman gave him a sharp look. "I can handle that matter too."

Slocum gave Darby and Shooter, who were headed to Fort Smith with the prisoners, thirty dollars from his own pocket.

Told them to take their saddles and to come back by train when they could. Then he rounded up the rest, who'd grabbed some food in a store, and they remounted their tired horses and headed back for home in the growing darkness.

Slocum hoped they did not meet Rensler and his men on the road. They could handle it, but he was so sleepy he could hardly hold his head up. A few hours out of Vinita at sundown, they moved off the road and found a sheltered place on the ground to grab some sleep, out of sight from the road.

Before noon the next day, he and his crew dismounted in camp and he hugged Katy. "Good to have you here."

"How did it go?"

"We captured or shot all of them. They are on their way to Muskogee, and then they will be hauled to Fort Smith."

"Wow, you did get lots done."

"There will still be problems. We burned all of Rensler's wagons. The railroad, I figure, will send in tough lawyers. But Marshal Hindman says that Judge Parker is not impressed by them."

She hung on his arm. "Have these men eaten anything?"

"Not since last night."

"I'll go tell Hoosie. We'll get something stirred up." She took off on a run.

The short cowboy, Alex, caught him. "You're still short-handed, ain't'cha?"

"I know, I should have left someone in Vinita to hire more help."

"I can go see where there might be some hands. Let me ride out to Enid."

"Think you can get some good men out there?"

"There's liable to be some hanging around out there."

"After we eat, get a fresh horse and go see." Slocum dug some money out of his vest. "We can hold most of it together. We'll need at least six more men."

Alex nodded.

"Be careful. I figure this bunch we're up against will want all of us all dead."

Alex nodded. "I'll be careful."

Slocum clapped him on the shoulder. "Get it done."

"I'll get a fresh horse and get out there now."

"Try to hire real ones."

"I know them." The short, bowlegged hand ran for the horse herd.

When she learned Alex was going for more help, Katy took him some food. He waved, and after he ate, he leaned out of the saddle to kiss her on the forehead and took off.

"Crazy cowboy." She came back shaking her head and looking a little red faced.

Slocum had a fresh cup of coffee and he laughed at her as she went by. "Guess you're on his special list."

"I sure didn't expect that." She went on by to help Hoosie.

How long would it take for Rensler to figure it all out? No way for Slocum to know for days. By then Rensler's men should be in the Fort Smith jail or else their lawyers would have a stay on the law. Rensler had too much to lose. If anyone in that crew testified about the cowboys' murders, they'd never stop the court from taking down Rensler and his whole operation.

The few hands Slocum had left rode out the next morning to turn the cattle back. Slocum had told them to be careful. He expected repercussions from Rensler, but he wondered when they would commence. With Rensler's loss of his guards and slaughter crew, he'd be shorthanded for any response with much force. In fact it might interrupt them from feeding the track crew. A smile swept over Slocum's face at the notion. Good enough for them.

He swept off his hat and went into the soddy. Katy greeted him. "What's so funny?

"Nothing. Just glad we're back to business." He hugged her. Hell, it was better knowing that many of those rustlers were in custody. Maybe he had ended his trouble, but he still knew Rensler wasn't through using his influence and the power of the railroads to push his weight around. There would be more trouble from him.

9

To Slocum's shock, the next day a little before midday Alex brought in six new hands from Enid and set the girls to fixing more food. They rode up on some nags and a few good horses of their own. That didn't matter; Slocum felt relieved to see them.

Alex had a small grin on his face when he leaned over the saddle horn. "We rode all night. These guys were all out of work. They were plumb excited to hear you needed help."

Slocum looked over his new help. "Welcome to the Triple A camp. My name's Slocum. We have lots of stocker cattle up here to look after. We spend our time keeping them in the lease's borders and keeping an eye on them so we don't lose them. If you run into any rustlers, do not try to handle them yourself. We lost two good men to them.

"I'll go buy you each a five-horse string. Till then you will use other men's horses. That's Hoosie, the cook, Katy, my lady, and Buddy. They handle the meals. Glad to have you here. Blue will cut you out some horses."

Then Slocum made a fast run to Vinita and lined up for Hank, the liveryman, to deliver him thirty-five horses at thirty bucks apiece. He filled out the check for $1,050 with a pencil on his saddle seat. The horses looked sound enough—he felt good about his purchases. To hell with Austin, he needed those men on horseback. Maybe even more men.

That evening with some hard riding, Slocum got back about the time the men came in. Alex introduced the new ones to the crew. "Meeker, he's the redhead. Josh is the roper of these men. Shallot here is the guy shorter than me. Realing is the bald one, Grant is the tall one, and Ferd is the Frenchman."

Then Alex introduced the other hands to the new men. Things were finally going smoother, Slocum decided.

Katy slipped up to him. "You must be worn out."

"I'll be fine. I did put some hard miles on Spook. I bought a few of those new ones for my own use."

"I'll go get you some food. Take a place," she told him, and frowned when he started to protest. In the end, he surrendered and she brought him a heaping plate of food.

"No word on Rensler in town?" she asked, scooting in beside him.

"Yes, there was. The liveryman, Hank, said they about had a revolt out at the end of the track—no beef to eat yesterday, and he said Rensler was trying to buy draft horses or mules and wagons. They were pretty excited about the whole deal. But the Vinita livery is holding the teams we brought in as federal evidence. I think there were half a dozen good teams there that he's missing. Plus some of his saddle horses."

"Good. I hope they lynch him for what he did to those two hands."

"I also think there are some flunkies in that bunch we shipped south that may have already sung like canaries before a grand jury about Rensler's activities. He might have to shake a leg out of here." Slocum shook his head.

"I hope so," she said. "Man, us taking care of these cattle has become a big deal. It's lots of work and costs money."

"We'll get paid. Then go on and do what we want. But I sure didn't hear a whisper about them Hudson brothers though. I'm wondering if they're working teams on slips up at the track laying."

"You better be careful going up there." She shook her head with concern in her eyes. "They may want you dead."

"I'll watch that."

10

New men and new horses—things went to popping the next morning. Some of the new cow ponies jammed their heads between their front knees and went off bawling like a pained hog when mounted. A few of the dismounts were like the lady at the circus coming out of the cannon with no net to catch her. Of course, the rest of the hands cheered the men on and threw coiled ropes and hats under the upset ponies to increase the activity. The activity proved to be a real dusty setup and some of the onlookers had tears in their eyes from laughing so hard.

Slocum watched the event from in front of the soddy with Katy under his arm. Both were tied up in laughter. He'd not seen such a scene in years. And the bucking must have become contagious, 'cause some of the other horses had fits too.

The wild riding must have lasted for ten minutes before everyone's horse was caught and snubbed up enough to allow every rider to climb back on and get a good seat. Several of the mounts "egg-walked," but new men paired with old were soon off for the day of findin, the stray cattle and sending them back onto the lease. A never ending job that kept the men in the saddle at least six days of the week. But

Slocum was satisfied his crew would eventually have the matter in hand.

Again he went back inside for one more cup of coffee and a look at the books.

"You have a big show out there?" Hoosie asked.

"Yes, a big show."

"No one get hurt?"

"They all looked all right when they rode out."

"They are all wonderful men," his cook said, busy rolling out pie dough.

"Oh, Hoosie, you're like me. You like all men that ain't mean and think they're all wonderful," Katy said.

"Maybe so. But if I knew that being a camp cook was going to be so much fun, I'd've been one lots sooner."

Katy joined her in pie making and Slocum got out the camp books, wrapped in oilcloth to keep dry, and brushed most of the dust out of the pages. Then with a straight ink pen and inkwell he went to work recording his expenses. He'd been working awhile when he noticed the light from outside had dimmed. Must be clouds coming in. But when he turned his ear to the rumble of distant thunder, he set down his pen, went to the door, and looked to the north. A huge, dark wall of clouds was advancing, and the lightning strikes were riding the advancing storm's face.

"Girls!" He stuck his head in the door of the soddy. "We need to grab everyone's bedding and get it in here in the dry. Where's Buddy?"

"Coming, boss man," he said, coming inside with an armload of split stove wood and dumping it on the floor near the range.

Slocum could feel the ground trembling under his boot soles as the storm approached. Grabbing up bedding and war bags, they tossed them into the soddy and ran back for more. The sulfur smell of lightning and the winelike aroma of rain on the dust in the air filled his nose.

Soon he and his three helpers had most of the gear inside, and the storm had arrived. They collapsed inside the building, out of breath. By then, he felt they had 90 percent of the things in out of the rain. Then hail went to beating on the cedar shingle roof, and looking out the door, he watched the quarter-size balls soon cover the ground. The temperature dropped twenty degrees. With the roar of the storm like a huge train passing over them, he hugged both women, who were holding their hands over their ears to muffle the sound. They literally were shaking under his hands. In flashes of lightning, he could see Buddy muffling his ears as well and sitting on his butt on the ground, trying to make it through the storm's blast of sound and fury.

Then it began to rain in great sheets. All Slocum could do was hope his men were all right. For the moment, the four of them here in camp were safe enough.

"Wish we had a fraidy hole," Katy said. "I'd even go sit in that dugout the last boss had up there."

"Pray a little for the good Lord to take care of us and the crew caught out in this mess. But we sure needed the water."

Katy agreed.

The rain kept up its onslaught and Slocum could imagine how the dry creek beds would soon be swollen with water. Flash floods caught many people unaware and swept them away. That notion worried him the most about his men when he thought about them out in it.

"When this lets up a little I'll go ride out and check on the crew."

"It don't sound like that will happen soon," Hoosie said, shaking her head. Both women sat at the table across from him, wringing their hands and looking around for the damage after every close lightning strike.

Thunder boomed and the ground shook some more. The bright flashes of lightning illuminated the room through the small windows. Falling temperatures made them hug their arms. Slocum finally lit a lamp and hung it overhead, busy wishing at the same time that the storm would move on.

Then the door flew open, and three drenched, masked men in slickers and armed with rifles burst into the room.

"Don't move a muscle," the leader shouted, pointing his long gun at Slocum.

Katy and Hoosie screamed. Rather than risk the two women being shot, Slocum rose with his hands in the air.

"You the cow camp boss?" the leader asked.

This intruder sure wasn't Rensler, but he had a tough enough edge in his voice with its air of authority to demand respect, backed by the long gun. They wore flour sack masks with eyeholes, and none were familiar. Their masks might keep them from being able to see clearly all around, but Slocum still considered them as dangerous as six-foot-long diamondback rattlers. One of them roughly jerked Katy off the bench.

"Leave her the hell alone," Slocum said.

"Hold it right there." The leader enforced his words by pointing the muzzle of his rifle at Slocum.

"You boys don't know who you're messing with," Slocum told him.

"It's you that don't know that. Messing with railroad construction can get you ten years in prison."

"Rustling cattle and murdering my hands can get you hung in federal court in Fort Smith. That's what that bunch of your fellows will get too."

"We're going to see about that."

"Judge Parker gets done with your outfit, you won't have one."

"Don't you threaten me, you son of a bitch." The leader poked his rifle at him. "If the boss didn't want to talk to you, you'd already be dead."

One of the men jerked Slocum's hands around to tie them behind his back. Ready for the maneuver, Slocum made his move and, with his left hand, jerked the man around in front of him as a shield. They'd made the mistake of not disarming him. His right hand was filled with his gun butt, the hammer cocked, and he shot the leader up close in the gut. The man's rifle went off at the ground before he crumbled to the floor. The man whose shirt Slocum held wadded up in his left fist screamed to avoid the same treatment. Man number three was on the floor, being kicked and hit by the two women and Buddy, who was armed with a stick of wood.

The gun smoke in the room was so smothering that the four of them were forced to drag the two invaders who hadn't been shot out into the deluge and make them stay belly down in the mud and running water while Slocum, Buddy, and the women stood at the wall under what passed for eaves.

"Who are they?" Katy asked, out of breath.

One by one, with his boot planted in the middle of their backs, Slocum jerked the masks off them. He didn't know either man. Soon Hoosie was kneeling beside the men on the wet grass. She grasped one guy's hair and jerked his head up while with her other hand, she held a butcher knife at his throat.

"Who are you, hombre? Tell me quick or you won't have an ear left."

"Garland O'Day."

"What's his name?" She indicated his partner.

"Loyd—" He swallowed hard. "Loyd Rowe."

"Who's your boss in there?" Slocum demanded.

"Art Layton."

"Who do you work for?" Slocum asked.

"The railroad—"

"Where's Rensler?"

"Springfield, Missouri, I think. He went up there anyway to talk to the feds."

"About getting his men out of jail, huh?"

Slocum shook his head at Hoosie to let him go and said to the man, "They have no authority in the Indian Territory. This is Judge Parker's ground. Rensler'll learn that fast. You two will too. I bet I can have you on tonight's train going down there."

About then two of his men rode up under slickers and stepped down, asking what had happened.

"Rensler sent three of his men up here to take me in for

questioning. One's dying inside, but the gun smoke is real bad in there."

Kelsey and Meeker nodded. They'd handle it. Then they went inside to drag the moaning man outside in the waning drizzle. Katy, under her own raincoat, brought Slocum his slicker.

"That was close, big man," she said.

"You three were great. Thanks." He hugged her shoulder. Her face grew red, and he saw that he'd embarrassed her. "Sorry, this was my problem, not yours."

"Hey, we're all in this together, big guy."

Hands started arriving. Buddy and Hoosie went inside to make some coffee. A couple of the hands used blankets to whip out some of the gun smoke from the soddy.

A sharp north wind swept over the rolling grassland, and the meadowlarks began to sing in the sunshine.

Slocum looked off to the northeast. What would they try next? Rensler wasn't through yet. Maybe a warrant for Rensler's arrest might set his butt in the federal jail under the courthouse down there. A slow smile crossed his lips as more of the crew rode in. He hoped that none were missing.

11

Everyone was back by five o'clock except Alex and a new man, Shallot. With several hours of daylight left, Slocum sent out parties to look for them. They'd gone southeast that morning, so the searchers went that way after some coffee and fried apple pies to tide them over till supper time.

Blue and the horses were still missing too, so Slocum and an experienced new man named Realing were going to look for him. Slocum'd borrowed another man's horse because his pony was out with Blue, so he tossed his rig on the animal's back. Cinched down, he rode northwest with the new man.

After a half hour, they spotted the Indian youth bringing in his herd.

"Plenty bad storm," Blue said when they caught up with him.

Slocum agreed and knew that was about all the Indian would tell them. The man, hardly more than a youth, would never say much. More horse than human in many ways, he was ideal for the job, but they'd never know what he'd gone through.

Slocum thanked him and they rode back to camp with the horses. He was hoping the others had found the two missing men—safe. Those two not coming in meant they'd had trouble. Coming out after Blue and the horses, he and Realing had crossed some wide, shallow water that flowed across where there wasn't even a dry wash cut in that area. On the way back, he could see the flow of that was fast dropping off.

At sundown, the lost ones, Alex and Shallot, were brought in. Lightning had killed Alex's horse out from under him and they'd had to swim two new rivers the rain had made. The pair took lots of razzing about their story but most of that came from the relief that everyone was all right, including Slocum.

The next day, Slocum and Katy hauled the dead man and two prisoners to Vinita. The head marshal, Ely Hindman, shook his head at the sight of Slocum and Katy at the hitch rack in front of his office. He acknowledged her with a tip of his hat.

"You'll be happy." Hindman said. "The two of your men are back from Fort Smith. Lucky for them they missed the two railroad bridges that washed out an hour after they crossed them."

"Good, I can use them." Slocum stepped down. "I brought you two more and a dead man who jumped us up in camp wearing masks in the middle of the storm."

"Come by before you leave town and fill out the papers." Hindman turned to two of his own helpers, who walked up at the sight of the prisoners, and said, "You two get them off those horses and then get that dead man down. We can lay him out here, and I'll have the undertaker come get him. Oh, yes, thanks, Slocum, they are still taking testimony from them other prisoners down at Fort Smith, according to my information."

He and Katy found the two men eating in the café that served good food. Both men hugged Katy and then sat down while Slocum told them about the raiders.

His men explained about the prisoners they helped deliver to Fort Smith. They'd been so anxious to cut a deal with the marshals that they all pointed their finger at Pauly as the one who shot the two cowboys while they knelt on the ground, which is just what Rensler had told them to do if they got found out rustling. Shooter ended with a headshake and said, "Me and Darby wanted to take Pauly out and tie him down on the tracks so a train could run over him alive."

"A couple of them tough ones wouldn't say anything," Darby said. "Just a handful. But they had it figured the outfit would get them off. Told us how powerful those railroads really were in Washington, D.C. Those deputies said, 'Don't listen to them. Judge Parker won't.'"

"Thanks. Did you hit the rain?" Slocum asked.

Shooter shook his head in dismay. "Yeah, we were on the train. They were stopping at all the bridges to check them before we crossed them. And later two washed out behind us."

"You two should have been in the soddy when all hell broke loose," Katy said.

They all laughed and went back to eating. Slocum left the ranch order at the store for Walking Bird to deliver, then they went back and filled out the necessary papers at the marshal's office about the attack. While he was doing that with Katy, the two hands went and picked out a couple of new horses at the livery to ride home, and then he'd add them to the remuda.

Back on the street, Slocum gave Katy a quick kiss, then they rode by the stables to get the others. He felt real good about things—especially the part about the warrant the head man at Fort Smith had sworn out for Rensler as the leader of the crime. With all the loose ends tied up for now, they headed home. The notion that the Hudson brothers might be working up there on the track end came to his mind. That was something that needed his attention, and that he had to get settled. No time that day to handle it though. He needed to have his hands count the losses from lightning and the cattle that were swept away if they could find any signs of them.

No word from Austin either. He must be real busy with that new woman in his bed. Of course, he knew all about that with Katy. But she was sweet as well as hot as a chili pepper. He pulled his hat brim down and told them to trot. Wouldn't be long till sundown, and he knew what that meant—more of the same. Maybe things would settle down after all that had happened. *Probably not really.*

12

Slocum woke up before the breakfast bell even rang. Sleeping in Katy's tent on the cot curled around her, he set his hand to wandering, and he squeezed her breast on the top side. She made a mumbled sound and then snuggled down deeper. He pulled up the short shirt she wore to sleep in and began to rub her rock-hard belly. More mumbling.

"Oh, that feels good." Then she raised her leg and reached between them to draw his erection up and inserted it inside her with some wiggling. He began to pump his rod into her a little at a time, bringing her into his action by massaging her breasts. Soon she was moist enough and they were into the process. At last he raised her up on her knees and reinserted his manhood from behind. Situated, he could reach under her and tease her rock-hard clitoris with his fingertip until she was blowing steam keeping up with him. Then he shot her full, and she near fainted at the end.

"Damn, you could set me off any way you want to." He let her down and she rolled over, spreading her knees apart for his entry.

"Yes, yes," she said in a drunken way. They were back into it. This time his fury had her gasping for breath, and his pubic bone was pressed to her pubic hair, and the rub was hot. In a short while he came again and she sighed, again close to fainting.

He rose up and then began to dress. "You coming?"

"I'm so split open, I may break in two like an egg."

"Whew, you are in tough shape."

"Not really, but I'm sore." Her hand shot to her crotch and she moaned. "I believe you could wear out a pile of us."

"Naw, you'll be ready for more by supper time." He could make out her shaking her head.

He tousled her hair. She laughed, then nodded. When he sat down to pull on his boots, she caught his mouth with hers and kissed the fire out of him. "There, you come back for more after supper."

"I will."

He wondered what Rensler would try next. If he had no influence on the court in Fort Smith, then he'd either duck and run or come back and try to take his business back over. No doubt the railroad was managing somehow, but not easily. Market centers for beef were not close by, and the supply might also be short. They couldn't use most trailed-in beef because it wasn't putting on weight fast enough to serve their needs. That meat would have to be boiled to be edible.

After breakfast and the crew had ridden out, Buddy, who saw the riders first, came running, shouting, "They're coming!"

Four riders in black suits and derby hats were headed in their direction. Slocum couldn't see if they carried rifles or not. He grabbed the Winchester by the door. Hoosie came running with two shotguns and handed one to Katy. Gasping for her breath, his cook asked, "More of them?"

"I'm not certain. You girls get under the chuck wagon. Don't pull the trigger until they start something. It may be something else."

Slocum didn't recognize any of them. They might be railroad security. They reined up at a safe distance and one large man nodded.

"We've come to talk business."

Slocum nodded, then waited with the rifle cradled in his arms. "You come in peace—fine. But don't try anything funny. We shot one man and took in the rest to the U.S. marshal yesterday."

The man dismounted, caught his derby so the wind didn't send it off, and handed one of the others his reins and head wear. Then, pressing down his wind-messed hair, he soon gave up on grooming and started toward him. "I'm Howard Blake, vice president of the Kansas City Iron and Steel Corporation, and I am here to buy beef."

"How does Rensler fit in with you boys?"

"He is no longer our beef supplier. We understand that he stole beef from you and also had some of your men murdered. But not on our orders."

"Rensler also later sent men here to kill me and my crew. That's why we're an armed camp and suspicious of anyone we don't know."

"I assure you that we had no knowledge of any of this until Marshal Hindman informed us of his dealings. He suggested, in fact, that we come out here and talk to you about becoming our new beef supplier."

"At the price Rensler offered to pay me, I'm sure not interested."

"Rensler was in the business to buy cheap. We are in need of an honest supplier with a ready supply of good beef. We have learned that just any old kind is not satisfactory. It's hard to keep good help working on tracks. And food is something important."

Slocum nodded. "Tell your men to get down. Hoosie, make us some coffee. We can get out of this wind and talk more inside."

"Thank you." Blake turned, invited his men to dismount and to hitch their horses.

Katy came out, set down the shotgun, and brushed the grass off her front. Slocum gave her a head toss to come along with them.

"That's Katy. My cook's name is Hoosie, and Buddy is my main camp man." The helper about busted his buttons off over Slocum's words.

"Don, Mark, and Carl," Blake pointed out the others with him.

Slocum was certain at least one of them was an agent. But they acted like businessmen and none looked gun happy, so he showed them inside.

They talked about a need for beef that amazed even him. Blake told him that workers could eat four to five pounds of good beef a day. The man also complained that the lack of buffalos along the right-of-way made rail building lots more expensive. During the conversation, the price of sixteen cents a pound on the hoof was brought up. The price sounded almost too good to Slocum.

"You're saying that you bought beef from Rensler for sixteen cents on the hoof?"

"Yes. Yes, and he assured us that he could keep us supplied at that price. Our goal is to keep those tracks being laid, and food is a main ingredient for that."

Slocum nodded. "I'll go into Vinita and wire my boss in Texas. I am certain he'd agree to furnish beef for that price. But we don't have the employees to butcher them."

"We can hire them. We simply need good beef on the hoof."

"Do you need beef right now?" Slocum met the man's steely gaze from across the table.

"Yes."

"Tomorrow afternoon we will have fifty head at the slaughter pens. That should be a two-day kill?"

"Mark, we can manage that, can't we?" Blake asked his man.

"Yes, we can have enough men ready."

"Good." Blake reached across the table and he and Slocum shook hands. The others smiled as if relieved and shook Slocum's hand as well.

Slocum sat back down. He was fixing to make Jake Austin

well off. This deal would beat anything he'd heard about in the cattle business. At this rate, Austin would need to start more cattle headed up here. In a few months, at this rate of kill, they'd soon be out of his cattle in the Indian Territory.

"My contract is with Kansas City Iron and Steel?" Slocum asked with his fingers tented.

"Right."

"How will we be paid? I know he'll ask."

"Weekly deposits to the Bank of Vinita all right?"

"Sounds good. I'll wire him and get you an answer as soon as possible."

"What do you think he'll say?" Blake asked.

Slocum frowned at the man. "What do you mean?"

"Do you think he will make the deal with us?"

"I imagine he will. Why?"

Blake sucked slightly on his eyetooth. "Good. We do need them."

"I can sell you at least that fifty head I mentioned. And by the time you need more, I'll have his answer."

Blake and his two associates nodded. "We'll get our men ready to butcher them."

Slocum turned to Katy. "Ride out northeast and find Darby. Tell him what we need. Fifty fat ones ready to drive to the rail camp in the morning. I'm going to Vinita to wire Austin. I should have an answer by the time the cattle get up there."

"Anything else?" she asked.

"Darby will know if he needs more men to drive them. Tell him to deliver them."

"You staying in Vinita tonight?" she asked.

Slocum nodded. "After you find him, come on down and meet me, either at the telegraph office or the hotel."

"I'll be there." She nodded to the four men, who had stood up for her, and she winked at Slocum. "Have a nice afternoon," she said to them and left on the run.

"Interesting young lady," Blake said.

"Some of my best help," Slocum said. "I better get on the way myself. I'll see you at the slaughter pens."

"I appreciate your cooperation," Blake said. "Unfortunate for both of us that Rensler's greed turned so violent. We are sorry about your losses and the men killed. As I said, it was not any plan of the company's, but his own ideas. We were paying him enough he had no need to steal."

"I understand." Slocum shook hands with the man again, and then with the other three. "I hope we have a good business relationship for a long time."

"So do we," the younger man said, with a weary shake of his head.

They all laughed.

Outdoors, Katy had brought around the two horses that had been saddled for the day in case they were needed. Slocum gave her a boost aboard and slapped her pony on the rump as she sped off.

He checked the cinch on his, nodded to Hoosie and Buddy, and swung into the seat. "You two are in charge."

"We can handle it." Hoosie said, beaming at him.

He watched his tomboy Katy headed northeast in a hard run. He waved at the railroad men ready to leave, and then he rode off to get to the telegraph office. He hoped that Austin was in town working so Slocum could get a reply as soon as possible. His boss'd never miss fifty head, but despite Slocum's idea that it was an extra fat deal, he wanted a nod from the man.

It was supper time when he rode into Vinita and dismounted at the wire office. Inside, the man under the celluloid visor looked up. "Yes sir?"

"I need to telegram my boss in San Antonio."

"I can do that for you."

Slocum picked up the lead pencil.

JAKE AUSTIN, SAN ANTONIO STOCKYARDS, SAN ANTONIO, TEXAS.

THE KANSAS CITY IRON AND STEEL BUILDING A RAIL LINE ACROSS THE NORTHERN INDIAN TERRITORY WANTS

US TO SUPPLY BEEF TO THEM LIVE AT SIXTEEN CENTS A
POUND. I SAID YES. THEY MAY SOON USE MORE THAN
THE HEAD I HAVE IN INVENTORY HERE. I WILL WIRE MY
NEEDS IF YOU APPROVE. SLOCUM

"Do you expect an answer?" the clerk asked.

"Yes. If I'm not here, I'll be at the King's Best Hotel. Get
me up if you need to."

"We can do that," he promised, asking for sixty cents for
the cost of the wire.

Slocum decided the process would require at least twelve
hours if Austin was in town. He waved to the telegraph man
and left the office to put his horse up at the livery. The street
was crowded with farm wagons, bicycles, horseback riders,
and several men in top hats. Other heads bore unshaped cowboy hats with eagle feathers trailing behind their owners like
wives who were wrapped in blankets.

He found Hank, the liveryman, who asked how the new
cowboys liked their job. The man took his reins.

"Fine, I guess. I've been too busy to ask." Slocum shook
his head in disbelief over that situation.

At that instant, he spotted the muzzle of a rifle at the side
of the harness and saddle shop that was pointed in his direction. "Get down."

He dove for cover, and the muzzle belched gun smoke.
On his belly with his gun drawn, Slocum thumbed off two
shots in the direction of the rifle he'd seen. Both shots chipped
wood off the corner of the building.

"You all right?" Slocum asked Hank as he struggled to his
feet.

"He never hit me."

The man who owned the harness shop ran outside. "Who
in the hell's shooting at my place?"

"Get back inside, Buster," Hank shouted at him. "There's
a crazy person over there shooting at us."

He obeyed as Slocum sprinted to the spot where the unseen sniper had been, six-gun in his fist. But the sound of

horses tearing off from behind the harness shop told him he should have gone mounted. The rider—or riders; he thought there was more than one—had rounded the corner, and they were already out of sight.

Behind the building, Slocum stopped a man. "You know them riders?"

The man, who was unloading some rolled-up leather hides for the shop, shook his head. "Never seen them two before. They damn sure lit out after the shots were fired."

"What did their hats look like?" Slocum holstered his gun. That might be a thing he could identify.

The man stopped and frowned. "One guy wore one that was torn in front like a dog had chewed on it."

Slocum nodded as Hank and the local law came running down the space between the shop and the building next door.

"Mister, you can't shoot your gun off in town."

Slocum shrugged. "Tell that to the ones who got away. They started it."

Hank tried to intercede. "There was a rifleman shooting at us."

The lawman shook his head wildly. "Don't matter. There ain't to be no shooting in the city limits."

Slocum looked up at his own hat brim for help. "Whoever it was, was shooting at us."

"I don't give a damn. The laws says—"

Hank shouted, "Emitt, Emitt, talk sensible!"

"Godamnit, you can't fire a firearm in the city limits. That's the law."

"Go arrest 'em," Slocum said, still wondering who'd taken the shot at him. He had enough enemies to fill a book with names. Starting with Rensler and his crew, whoever was left of them, plus the Hudson brothers if they were still in the country and had gotten wind of Slocum's pursuit. Maybe someone else affected by the loss of the beef contract wanted revenge. No telling, but he'd be a damn sight more aware from there on.

He apologized to Emitt to soothe the man. Then he went back across the street with Hank.

"I never saw their faces," the liveryman said. "Lucky he missed us and your horse."

Slocum shook his head and chuckled. "All three of us are lucky we aren't in jail together with my horse charged as an accessory."

"Aw, Emitt means well. He just gets all fired up when folks go to wild shooting. I think the city council warned him if there was any more of it they'd fire him."

"Thanks. I may have to stay here for a few days to clear up my business. Grain my horse. I might have some hard riding to do."

"We can handle it."

"Meanwhile, I'm going to stay at the King's Best Hotel, and I expect Katy to join me and put her horse up here too."

"No problem. Not to be smart, but she sure is a looker." He shook his head as if impressed.

Slocum agreed and headed for a meal. He hoped, striding the boardwalk, that Austin would answer him in a hurry. He doubted that the man would be angry over the proposed contract—by Slocum's calculations it could be a very profitable deal for him.

Inside the café, he checked the wall clock. Six-thirty. He took an empty table with a nod from the gal waiting on other customers. "Be right with you, sir."

"Fine." Seated, he could wonder about Katy and how successful she had been finding Darby. By this time she should be on her way to town or close. She wouldn't waste any time getting here, especially with a nice bed at the hotel waiting for the two of them.

He was finishing his meal when a red-faced boy wearing one-strap overalls burst into the room.

"Th-they said you wasn't checked in, Mr. Slocum." He handed Slocum a telegram and proudly hung on to the one strap with both hands waiting for his word.

SLOCUM, SOUNDS GREAT. MAKE THE DEAL. SEND ME A
LETTER ON CONDITIONS. JAKE

"Want to send a reply?"

"I will write one out for you to send."

On a used sheet from his pocket, he wrote out his reply in pencil.

SHIP FIRST 50 HEAD TOMORROW. PAY IN A WEEK DEPOS-
ITED IN THE BANK HERE. LETTER TO FOLLOW. JS

"Here's the money for the wire," he said, placing the two quarters for the wire. "The extra quarter is for you."

"A whole quarter? Wow." He stared at silver coins in his palm. "You got any more wires coming? I'd sure bring them fast."

Slocum grinned and shook his head. "Good."

The boy tore off, and Slocum went back to eating his supper. Going out the door, the boy about swept Katy away. Pleased to see her, Slocum stood up and removed his hat to wave her over.

"Who was that?" she asked.

He motioned for her to take a seat and handed her the paper. She looked up from reading it. "Austin already likes our deal. Boy, wires on the line go fast."

"I'd say so. And he's in San Antonio?" she asked, looking amazed as he sat her down.

"Yes, wonderful invention."

"Faster than lightning." She shook her head. "Oh, Darby said he could deliver the cattle. He was excited. Said that should make work for the entire crew for a long while."

He agreed, then ordered her a meal, and the waitress brought it right back.

"It will make work for them boys. Oh, yes, and someone shot at me from cover this afternoon right here in town."

"Oh, my God. I'm glad he missed."

"So am I. What'cha looking for?" He couldn't figure out why she was acting so nervous about looking all around.

"I want to get out of here."

"You haven't eaten half of your meal."

She shook her head to dismiss his concern. "I'll tell you later. I'm not hungry."

He left the money and a tip on the table and hurried after her as she headed for the hotel. At the front desk, he told the night clerk to give her the key to the room and for her to go on up to room—

"Twenty-seven. Turn right at the top of the stairs."

"I can find it. See you up there." She rushed up to the room and he filled out the registry: Mr. and Mrs. John Howard.

Slocum thanked the young man and went after her. What was wrong with her? He turned the knob and opened the door, and she was lying naked on her back atop the bed.

"Get undressed," she said, holding the back of her hand to her forehead. "I been thinking about screwing you all day long and I am completely obsessed with the idea. I itch so bad inside, I think I'll scream."

When he was undressed, he crossed the room to get inside her outstretched arms. "Oh, save me. . . ."

He'd known other women to be real horny before, but she beat them all. He got on his knees on the bed and aided his oncoming erection a little with his hand. As soon as he was stiff enough to enter her, he waded across the bed to get between her slender parted legs and hoisted his erection inside her wet gates. Ready enough for his entry, she threw her head back and cried out. "Oh, thank you, God. That feels so damn wonderful."

She moaned and groaned. Cried out loud as he increased the tempo. With each stroke, she humped her skinny ass at him time and time again. Then the muscular spasms inside her began to wrench on his tender, thin-skinned hard-on. He felt the tight knob on the end of his shaft begin to tingle and an unseen hand crush his nuts. In an instant, he came inside her with the fury of a rifle shot and it cut off her screaming. But he knew it wasn't enough. Never enough.

Sprawled on her back, she moaned softly. "That was better than I ever dreamed it would be. Oh, if anything ever happened to you, I think they would have to put me in the crazy house, I'd be so damn horny. We once had a billy goat that went so mad for sex, he bred five nannies in a row, and two of them weren't even in heat. Didn't matter to him how much they bleated and pleaded for him not to, he screwed each one of them till creamy cum ran out of them like blood. Man, he was horny."

He pulled her knees apart and started to get on her again. "You comparing me to a goat?"

"No, you're better than that." Then she hunched up her small ass to accept his shaft. "Lots better." And they were reunited—again.

After the third time, she collapsed and fell asleep instantly. He curled around her and inserted his dick inside her—that would do her for a while.

He recalled one time being caught alone in a heavy rain in Mississippi during the war and finding a large unburned house. Grateful for the shelter, he knew the message he bore could wait and decided to sit out the storm in the dry interior. Seated on the hardwood floor, because all the furniture had been ransacked and stolen, he unbuttoned his canvas long coat and heard a noise.

A woman was coming down the broad stairs in a lacy nightgown. She called out, "Albert? That you?"

"No, ma'am—"

She never stopped descending the steps. "Oh, Albert, you're home at last."

When she reached the bottom flight, she rushed over and hugged Slocum. "Oh, where have you been for so long, my darling?"

She was delirious. He damn sure wasn't Albert. But what the hell, why not, so he kissed her. Made no difference to her. She had long, tubelike breasts and flowing brown hair. He guessed her to be in her midtwenties. Nothing to do but enjoy his good luck. He kissed her again. This time he pulled the pink ribbon bow that kept the gown up and the garment dissolved downward. He stepped over to hold her smooth, bare body to him and kissed her, tongue and all.

"Is there a bed left?" he whispered and swept her up in his arms.

"One is all," she said dreamily.

He noticed in a glimpse that she had some stretch marks on her belly. He wondered where her children were at. The stairs weren't difficult to go up, carrying her in his arms. He found the high bed like an unscathed island in the midst of the dusty hardwood floor in the bedroom, with some gauzy curtains swaying from the wind and the rain outside.

He laid her on the bed and began to undress. Like an upset person, she rolled from side to side on top of the sheet. Naked, he joined her in the bed and kissed her while he probed with his finger for her clit until he could pinch the small erection between his fingers.

"I'm ready," she slowly whispered. And he climbed aboard.

As he struggled to enter her, she said, sounding drunk, "You can't get your knee in me, Albert."

"It's not my knee, dear." He spoke softly into her ear.

"Oh, it sure feels like it. Remember, don't go too deep, not past my ring, my love."

"Yes—"

His hard probe finally slid past her ring and her fingernails were clawing his back like she'd never experienced anything like it—such deep penetration. But she was so swept up in their performance she must have never noticed his depth as she moaned in pleasure. Her face got lost in her brushed brown hair.

"I never let a man go that deep inside me in my life, not even you, Albert. But I thought I was having a baby again. Oh, had I known—my, my."

When at last he came and after his dick slipped out of her, she rose up on her elbows and blinked at him, shaking the hair out of her shocked face. "You aren't Albert, are you?"

"Never said I was."

"Wait, don't leave me. He won't be home till supper time."

She dropped on her back and held out her arms for him to come down on top of her again. "Forget I ever called you that. Can we do it again? I mean, can you go that deep inside me again?

"Oh, I sound like such a slut, but I haven't had sex like that since I did it with a black person when I was a teen. He was special. If he'd been white, I'd've married him. But even he never went that deep. I hated being pregnant. So uncomfortable, and that big belly of mine, why, Albert could only go in an inch deep when I was that bloated. He's very short down there. That was why I married him. I had no plans to be pregnant all the time. But you don't want to talk about that, do you?"

He hoisted his hardening hose back inside her gates. "Where are your children?"

"Under tombstones. They both had the fever and died quickly. I think I'll have one more by you so I have some company. That damn Albert may not come back. War and all. Ooooh, that feels wonderful."

He spent twenty-four hours with her and couldn't even recall her name. "The lady in the big house with no furniture" was how he recalled her. He wondered if she ever had another baby and where she was at. Cuddled around his hatchet-assed companion, he smiled to himself. Katy was something else. Then he went over the things he needed to handle.

Cattle delivery would be in twenty-four hours. They'd better go up there to the weighing-in next and watch that operation. Austin would be dying to hear the results of the first sale. Slocum would wire him as soon as he knew the outcome. And then he'd write Austin a letter; there was a small stationary store in Vinita. He'd seen the sign on Main Street as he was riding in there. Then he drifted off to sleep.

In the morning they had another round of thumping each other before sunup, and then they each took a spit bath with the bowl and pitcher on the dresser before pulling on their clothes. They were in the café eating breakfast when the sun began to purple the eastern horizon. The hot coffee tasted heavenly, and Katy winked at Slocum over the cup's rim.

"You never told me where you live," she said.

"Wherever I sleep."

She shrugged her narrow shoulders and turned her attention back to her plate. "I guess that suits you?"

"Are you asking me if I want to settle down and live on a farm?"

"Well—" She looked at him for a long second. "I simply wondered if you ever would do that."

He shook his head. "I've got too big a sugar foot to ever do that."

"Yeah, you sleep wherever you lie down. If you don't have something to cover first." Then she blushed. "Like me."

He laughed and asked the passing waitress what time the stationary store opened. The gal, a woman in her forties and kinda soggily made, stopped and smiled at both of them. "Oh, I guess eight o'clock or so. You need some paper and an envelope, I can find you some and a pencil. Wait till I get some more coffee poured and I'll get it for you."

"No rush." He thanked her and she went on.

"Who're you going to write to?" Katy asked.

"Austin. Explain the deal so he knows all about it."

She nodded and wiped her mouth on the napkin. "How much education do you have?"

"Oh, enough. My father planned to send me to advanced military school, but then the war broke out. That put the lid on that. Why?"

"Just nosy, I guess." She cradled the cup of coffee in both hands. "I could write a letter. Maybe. Spelling might be bad. But how do you write a letter like you're going to write him?"

"Simply tell him what's happening and how the deal was made."

She nodded and lowered her voice. "Suppose Maw would like to read what we're doing?"

"She might." About then the waitress delivered the pencil, paper, and envelope to Slocum.

"Need anything else, we've got more."

"Thanks very much." He moved his empty plate aside.

"Aw," Katy said privately. "She'd think I was simply bragging, telling her how many times a day we've been doing it. She don't need to know either."

They both laughed. He began writing the letter telling Austin how he made the deal. How many head he expected to sell the railroad every other day and the need to line up more stock for later. In just over four months he'd have all these cattle sold to the construction company. He wrote of how the Bank of Vinita would handle the payments and that he, Slocum, would talk to them before the first payment arrived. The same outfit held his ranch account. When he finished, he signed off and handed the letter to Katy.

She read it aloud in a low voice and shook her head. "Sounds just like you. I see now how to write one, like I talk. Good, I'm learning."

He paid for the meal, giving the waitress a good tip, and she took his letter to mail it for him since the post office was not open that early. At the livery, Hank was still sleeping when his hustler brought out their horses and they saddled them.

"Land sakes," Hank said, putting up his suspenders and coming out in the first light. "You two get up early enough, you don't miss sunup."

They laughed.

"I see he found you. I was sure hoping you'd get lost, Miss Katy, and I'd have to board you here till he got back." They laughed as the man stretched, trying to get more awake.

With their horses saddled at last, Slocum booted Katy up on her horse and then swung up on his own. "Not today, Hank. We'll see you sometime later."

"I'd sure look after her real good."

Katy shook her head, smiling, and they rode off for the slaughter pens. It was not quite noon when they arrived. A man named Tennet met them. He was in charge, and the newly employed butchers came out to see who they were and to peek at Katy between sharpening their long knives.

"They going to be here with the cattle today?" Tennet asked Slocum as they squatted on their boot heels under the canvas tent cover, which was popping in the wind.

Slocum nodded. "Darby will have them here by afternoon."

"You and she can come up to the cook area. We'll drink some coffee while we wait."

Katy wrinkled her small nose at Slocum. "I'll ride in that direction and let you know how far out they are."

"Good. Be careful." He went along and boosted her aboard. She threw him a kiss, turned the horse, and left in a lope.

The coffee was fresh and they talked about slaughtering beef. Slocum explained that the cattle had been putting on lots of flesh on the rich grass. Soon Blake arrived and asked about the cattle.

"Katy went to see about them. I imagine they'll soon be here. We were in town last night and my man Darby is bringing them up."

"Good enough. I couldn't stand another day of complaining by the workers up there. They may eat me out of house and home when the beef does arrive."

"Good, I have more. You haven't heard where Rensler is at?"

"Not a word. The company is charging him with falsifying receipts for payment as well."

"Good. Maybe we can throw away the key."

"I hope so. This has been a big mess."

Before the sun time turned to noon, Katy came short loping back to the pens. Flush faced, she slipped off her horse, and one of the men took the reins from her.

"They're about an hour out," she said and joined Slocum and the man.

Blake looked relieved, and they sat back on the benches as the cook rang the bell and everyone came to eat.

"How many of your hands are coming?" the head cook asked Slocum.

"Six," Katy said. "Darby wanted to be sure they arrived so he has two extra men."

"I'll have enough food for them too," the head cook said and went back to work.

"Thanks," Slocum said, and some kitchen help brought the three of them each a loaded tin plate with a couple of oven-brown biscuits capping the top of them.

"Wow, the service is sure nice here," Katy said to Blake.

"Can't be good enough for you all. You've saved my neck."

When they finished their meal, the sounds of bawling cattle began to resound across the prairie. The first job was about over and the tradition started.

In scaling the fifty head, they found they weighed 730 pounds apiece. At sixteen cents a pound, they brought Austin $5,840. Slocum was impressed. At that price they brought almost $117 a head. In Texas, they had probably cost Austin less than $20 a head six months earlier.

They shook hands around the table when the yard man came by and bragged on the flesh condition of the cattle to Blake, who looked even more relieved over that fact.

On horseback, Darby stopped by with a big, wide grin. "How many will you need day after tomorrow?"

"Plan on fifty more. He'll get us word if he needs more than that," Slocum said. "You boys better get to gathering."

"Where are you headed?" Blake asked Slocum when Darby rode off.

"Back to Vinita to wire Austin about how well his cattle sold."

Blake grinned, "You might be a hero with him too. Good to see you again, Katy." He tipped his hat to her.

Slocum could have sworn she blushed. They left for Vinita.

"One good thing," she said under her breath when they were out of hearing. "We can use one of those hotel beds again tonight."

They arrived in Vinita about sundown, put their horses up,

and washed up at the pump out in front of the livery. Then they went to the café. Hank waved them over to where he sat by himself.

"How did the sale go?"

"Fine," Slocum said. "They were pleased. I'm certain my boss will be as well."

Hank looked around the room, then when he looked satisfied, he said, "Two deputies from Kansas were in here today asking lots of questions about you."

Slocum's heart stopped as he searched the room. No familiar faces were in the place. His heart thumped under his breastbone like a sledgehammer. How long since he'd thought they'd given up pursuing him? A couple of years? He wasn't certain.

"Was one of them riding an Appaloosa horse with a blanket ass?" Slocum asked.

Hank nodded. "What do they want you for?"

"Shooting a guy. A long time ago I was playing poker in Fort Scott, Kansas. A young man foolishly lost lots of money and, drunk, left the card room swearing to get even over his losses. Sounded like whiskey talk. Liquor was illegal in Kansas then. He left and came back threatening to shoot me. He pointed a gun at me and hesitated. I drew and shot him. His grandfather was rich and powerful. He had me charged with murder, and for several years he paid the expenses of those two brothers to chase me. It finally petered out, and I thought it was all clear. Guess that was too good to be true. Where did they go?"

"I guess out to the cow camp. Someone probably told them where you were at."

He nodded at Hank. "I'll have to take a powder. Darby can handle the job out there. I'll just have to dodge them."

"What can I do to help you?" Hank asked. "Hell, I was just getting to the point of liking you."

Katy laughed.

"I need to get word to Darby that he's going to be in

charge of the deal from here on and wire Austin that my welcome wore out here."

"What'll he do? Austin, I mean."

"Hell, he's known about my problem with those two for years. He'll trust whoever I put in charge."

"Missy," Hank said. "You ever need a roof or a friend, I'll show you a good time, and you sure got a place to stay if you need one with me."

"We'll see. But thanks, Hank."

"Yes, ma'am. I ain't trying to steal ya. Just want you to know you'd have a good place here with me if you ever need it."

She nodded and thanked him.

"Thanks, Hank. Katy you bring the horses, we'll eat later," Slocum said and headed for the front door. The telegraph office was a block away on foot. He figured Hank had been speaking straight enough to her.

He sent the message to Austin.

Austin, have to leave. Darby can handle the cattle. Good man. All is well up here otherwise. 50 cattle sold for $5,840. Slocum

When he came out of the office, Katy smiled. She had his horse in tow and handed him the reins. "Where to next?"

"The cow camp," he said in a low voice.

"But—"

"They won't be there all day if we ain't there. We can swing around, come in from the north, and not meet them on the road."

"I understand."

So they short loped for a ways to miss the deputies. Found a small playa and rolled out the bedroll. With the horses watered and hobbled, Slocum and Katy chewed on some jerky under the stars and washed it down with canteen water. Then they took on undressing and forgetting about how close the law had gotten to them.

At dawn they were up and rode on to where they could

look at the cow camp from a distance. With their horses out of sight, he took out his field glasses and scoped the camp from a rise. The south wind was whipping the grass stems around in their faces where they lay belly down in the forage as the light spread out over the cow camp. As he expected, there was no Ap horse around the chuck wagon. Nothing from the east. His pursuers had already left.

"Let's go, Katy," he said, getting up on his knees.

"I don't want those deputies to get you."

He put his arm around her. "They won't get me, but soon I'm going to need to ride out of this country."

She whirled and frowned at him. "Leave me?"

"Darling, sometime I warned you we'd have to part. I can't dodge those men and keep track of you too."

"Oh, Slocum, you can't simply ride off."

"Before I leave, I'll cut you a check from Austin's account big enough that, if you manage it right, you can live good for six months on it."

"But I don't need money, I need you."

"You'll understand someday. Did you hear my friend offer you a deal yesterday?"

"He won't be the same."

"Then go back to your mom's."

She slapped her forehead. "No, I can't do that. That would be so damn boring. I could just cuss, I am so upset."

"Baby, I don't like it either, but it's the cards we drew in life."

"What about those brothers?"

"The Hudson brothers? Oh, I'll get them. They only have a short time to live."

"Let me go with you?"

"Too dangerous. After we see Darby, I'm tracking out of here."

She frowned hard at him. "Where will you go?"

"I'm not certain."

"Damn you, you won't tell me. I'm going to cry."

"Don't do that. I never beat you."

"Same thing, leaving me."

"I simply have to." She went along with him into the camp, then she left him to go find Hoosie and Buddy.

Darby came to greet him. "Who were those damn deputies come out here looking for you? Cussing bunch. I told them I run this camp and for them to just stay the hell out."

Slocum explained their part in his life and his problems. He told Darby to write Katy a check for $400 to cover his and Katy's wages. Austin wouldn't care. Slocum had made that much or more off the first bunch of cattle he sold for him.

"The bank will take your checks. Just be fair and honest with the man." Slocum sat down and wrote a note to the man at the bank that Darby would be in charge of the Triple A cow camp and that he, Slocum, had had to leave unexpectedly.

Slocum had Blue go catch his horse, Spook, and then he took Katy aside to speak to her privately. "Darby is going to pay you four hundred bucks, and that will take you a long ways. I've had a helluva time."

"I'd rather have you."

"What did she say about the liveryman?"

"Hoosie?"

When he nodded, she said, "She thinks he's a super nice man."

He winked at her. "Take a conditional honeymoon with him. He don't work out, you cut a trail."

"Damn you. I'm still mad."

He hugged and kissed her, then stood her back in place. Blue had brought in his horse and was changing saddles. "You're a wonderful woman, Katy. Ride easy."

"I won't forget you."

"Naw, you'll find a better one." He winked at her, then thanked Blue, taking the reins. "See you, Katy."

She shook her head and turned her back on him to pout. He looked back and shook his head, then rode off.

By dark he was across the Kansas line. When it threatened

to rain, with distant lightning flashes in the west, he stopped. A rancher let him sleep in a shed. In the morning the droplets of water on the grass looked like diamonds. He thanked the rancher and his wife and rode on. His plans were to make a large circle to lose the Fort Scott lawmen and get back to the railroad area to see if the Hudson brothers were working on the track crew.

By evening he was in the temporary boomtown. Obviously the saloons had been closed down by order of the U.S. marshals, according to the signs nailed on the doors. The only liquor being sold was slyly purchased from a wagon covered by a tarp. When Slocum edged close, a man with a mustache who was leaning on the side of the rig and busy whittling asked what he needed.

"Got a little whiskey?"

"Two bucks."

"Kinda steep, ain't'cha?" Slocum complained.

"You must be new here. Them damn marshals closed us down, and even the railroad couldn't get us reopened."

After looking around, he finally slipped the half pint out and took Slocum's money.

"Thanks," Slocum said, putting it inside his shirt. "There's some guys I know working up here. Randle and Ulysses Hudson. You know them?"

"Yeah, they just bought two bottles not a half hour ago and went to Rose's tent, to get a little, I guess."

"Well, hell, we can have a real reunion then. Thanks, pard."

He started across the road leading Spook. He intended to walk right into that cat house and take them two out feetfirst or alive, whichever they chose. He climbed the stairs and heard some gal shout, "Wait! You ain't paid me!"

Dumb girl. Why, you ought to know to collect beforehand— then he heard another shout and some fellow fell out of a second-story window in the back. There was shouting, cussing, and confusion all over the place. Slocum made the stairs in a two-at-a-time chase and only his quick dodge saved him from being run down by two buxom females who were scantily clothed, headed like a freight train down the stairs.

Gun in his fist, he looked around in the screaming confusion for either of the two men he was searching for. A woman waved him over to her doorway. "You want that sniveling sumbitch?"

Slocum stopped short of the door and let her slip aside. Holding out his wrists, and naked save for some holey underwear about to slip off his narrow hips, stood Ulysses Hudson.

Slocum ran by him and looked out the window to see a rider fanning the breeze to get out of there. "Is that Randle got away?"

"I guess, I guess."

"Get dressed," Slocum ordered. "And don't you try one thing."

"Oh, I won't. I won't."

Well, he damn sure better not try to make one wrong move.

"Howdy, big guy." The woman came over and put her arm on Slocum's shoulder. "You and me, baby, need to get in that bed and grind away a little at it."

"Maybe another time. How did his brother get out of here?" Slocum asked, hardly attracted by her rolls of fat.

"He wasn't in here. He was next door—"

"He was in my room," said a brassy redhead with bare breasts like melons and who was posing herself in the doorway. "The woodshed broke his fall. You must be one tough sumbitch to scare them two bastards that bad."

"They murdered a friend of mine in Texas," Slocum said, herding his now-dressed prisoner with a head toss in her direction.

"You going to lynch him here?" Red asked.

"Naw, I'm shipping him back to Texas and let him sit there, waiting for his hanging for a while."

"Hell, we'd all like to see a real necktie party, wouldn't we, girls?" Red asked the dozen or so women clustered with some of their customers on the upstairs landing.

"No, too easy for him." Slocum said and marched the man downstairs. "Where's Randle headed?"

"How the fuck should I know?"

"You know damn good and well where he's headed. You better tell me, or I'll put a noose around your neck and make you walk to Vinita. And I might even drag you part of the way."

"Ogallala."

"Why up there?"

"Our sister lives up there."

"What's her name?"

"Penelope."

"Penelope what."

"Granger."

"Hold up." Slocum caught his sleeve to stop him. Then he turned to look up at all the painted faces upstairs. "Ladies, thanks for helping me get him."

"Come back, cowboy, and I'll give you a ride you won't ever forget," some blonde shouted back and then shook her bare boobs at him.

"Me too." Another promised the same.

He sent Hudson on and smiled. Damn, leaving that Katy was a pure shame when he considered those sloppy ones working upstairs. Whew, their strong perfume was burning his nose. He sneezed twice going out the door behind Hudson.

Hours later in the dark, he slipped into Vinita and took his prisoner to the U.S. marshal's office looking for Hindman. He quickly explained to the deputy in charge who Hudson was and told him to wire Sheriff Taylor in Hilton County, Texas, who'd send a man up there for him.

"You all can share the hundred bucks reward on this one, and also take his horse and the rest. His brother has hotfooted it for Nebraska, and I want to meet him there."

"Good luck, Slocum. I'm sure Marshal Hindman would like to be here to thank you too," the deputy said.

Slocum nodded, then left the office and Vinita. His back

itched all the way out of town, feeling like the Kansas deputies were somewhere close by—too close. Off in the night, a coyote yipped at the moon. Hell of a note to lose Katy's wonderful company and replace it with a mangy damn coyote—but that was his luck.

13

In York, Nebraska, four days later, he sold Spook to a livery, and with his saddle and war bag on his shoulder, he climbed on the second passenger car of the 4:06 westward bound. The conductor had him store his gear in the back area by the cold stove, and he moved forward to take a seat by a woman he spotted who appeared to be in her late twenties. With light brown hair in long curls, she held in her lap a wide-brim hat with flowers that looked real on it. Prim and proper–looking, she inched over with a soft "No problem" when he took off his hat and asked if she minded company.

"Thank you, ma'am," he said and sat down.

"Your mother must have been a strong-minded woman," she said, looking out the window at the yellow and brown depot and acting like she didn't dare look over at him.

"How is that?"

"Most hooligans would have sat down and moved me over." Then she laughed as if embarrassed at her own frankness.

"Glad I'm not in that class."

"You aren't? Do you usually wear spurs?" She peered over at his dusty toed boots.

126

"Yes, ma'am. But since I can't hurry this train none, I left them in my saddlebags."

"I'm glad. I'd've hated to have been spurred on this trip."

If she'd give him half a chance, he'd sure spur her. Straight backed, she certainly made a good-looking woman. "No danger of me doing that today."

"Are you a stockman?"

"Have been. I was supervising about three thousand head on a lease down in the Indian Territory for a man from San Antonio."

"Did you quit? You don't look like a man who would be fired from any job."

"I had to quit. A man who killed a good friend of mine down in Texas is supposed to be in Ogallala. I'm headed there to find him."

"Oh." The way she made her full red lips into a circle made him realize he'd sure like to taste her mouth.

She responded with, "Isn't that dangerous? I mean going after a killer."

"Life is a dangerous place anyway." He shrugged the notion away. "He killed a family man with a good wife. He doesn't deserve to live."

"Will you just shoot him down whenever you find him?"

"I captured his brother. He surrendered when I came in the room he was in."

"I would too." She snickered and shook her head. "Was he wearing a gun then?"

He considered his answer, recalling the nervous Hudson in his underwear, about to pee in them. "No, ma'am. I snuck up on him and caught him away from his gun."

"I thought men like that slept with their weapons."

"He wasn't wearing it. But when his brother discovered I was there, he jumped out of a second-story building and rode away."

"Where is the man you captured at?"

"In the Vinita jail, soon to be taken back to Texas for trial, or possibly already on his way. I'm trying to beat his brother to Ogallala."

"Are you a lawman as well?"

"No, just a citizen."

"Well, with all these outlaws we read about in the West, you are a sterling citizen."

He shook his head. "Just doing the right thing."

"You are a very modest man. Allow me to introduce myself. My name is Mrs. Lea Malloy."

"Slocum's mine. Nice to meet you, Lea."

"No, sir. It is my pleasure."

"You know where I came from. Where do you live?" he asked her.

"Cheyenne, right now. My husband, Thomas, is having a residence built on our ranch up in Douglas."

"You have a ranch up there in Douglas?"

"Yes. Have you ever been there?"

"Yes, ma'am, but only in passing. You like the country?"

She mildly shook her head. "Why would a woman who has lived in Eastern society all her life enjoy such isolation? I don't want to be there. What can I do at the ranch but prance around my living room?"

He snickered. "You would, if I may say so, look quite attractive doing that."

She looked at the train car ceiling for help. "What do you do in such a place?"

"I'd go to every country dance and dinner I could find. There is one at every schoolhouse in the land on Saturday night out here."

"What do I need to bring?"

"Food or dessert, and don't outdress them."

"Oh, well, when I get there, I'll be at every one of them, as you suggested. And I understand how not to overdress. I am in your gratitude, sir. I shall go to every one I can find."

"These working people know how to have a good time. Different, maybe, than what you're accustomed to, but in Rome you must do as the Romans do."

"Thank you, Caesar."

She recrossed her legs and settled her skirt. With her legs crossed, her high-button shoe swung idly out from under the hem. "I never expected to find such interesting company on a public coach. Thomas usually uses his private railcar, but I stayed over in New York when he came back earlier to oversee the house construction. I dismissed his concern and told him that other people ride public railways all across the nation unharmed. He said, 'Well, it's your neck.'"

Slocum nodded, looking out of the car and thinking about all the farmers that were plowing under the waving grass outside of the smudged window. A cowman's dream being turned roots-up for progress. Rich grazing land that had once fed the huge waves of buffalo that would pass for days, according to the tales of the early settlers. He noticed several sod houses on these homesteads as the train streamed west at twenty-five miles per hour—the legal federal speed limit.

"We will be in Ogallala," she said, looking at the timetable she drew from her canvas bag, "at approximately 3 A.M."

"Eleven hours, that's about right." He wondered what that meant. Faster than the long-expired pony express anyway.

"I think I will stay there for a day to rest up. Take a bath. It's hard for me to sleep sitting up. Is it wild there?"

"Some. It's becoming a real cow town fast-like."

"They say Cheyenne is like that too. However, I found most of you Western men polite."

"Most are."

He slipped down in the seat and used his hat to shade his face as the sun sank lower in the west. His ears were open for her melodic voice and he was waiting for the spinning roulette wheel in his brain to stop. Would she invite him to share such a place? No telling. She might just be open to such an adventure with him.

"I guess you can find a room at that hour?" she asked him casually. "You know, single women are sometimes mistaken for women of the night and are refused a room."

She had slid down in the seat as well to be beside him and

was talking in a low whisper. "What if we check in as——"

"As Mr. and Mrs. John Howard?" he asked and she squeezed his hand very carefully.

"Exactly. Then I'd have no worries." She put her hat on and hid behind the brim.

"None whatsoever, Mrs. Howard." This could prove interesting, he decided, and tried to draw a mental picture of what she would look like under her travel wear: a full denim skirt, a ruffled white blouse, and formfitting vest.

"Lean over." She raised the brim of her hat, and when he appeared from under his own, she quickly kissed him on the mouth, then ducked back down.

"Whew." She settled back beside him with her arms folded over her chest. "This is heady."

"You might be disappointed."

"I doubt it."

"We'll see." He closed his eyes under his own hat.

The train, they learned from the conductor, would arrive on time. Slocum took his saddle and war bag and the porter took Lea's two bags to the exit at the end of the car to prepare for debarking. Most of the scattered passengers remained asleep on the uncomfortable benches.

Slocum told the porter they needed a taxi. The black man nodded. "I's knows a good one here."

Slocum slipped the black man a silver dollar, and the man nodded, acting impressed at his generosity. "We be there soon. Hold on," he said as the train's air brakes began to make the steel wheels slide on the tracks with a squeal.

The conductor went down first and put down the step. Slocum set down his saddle and war bag on the dock, then helped the lady off the stairs, and the porter descended with her bags.

The porter waved to a man who hurried over and bowed. "Chester Brown at your service."

"The best hotel," she whispered wifelike to Slocum.

"The best hotel in town," Slocum told him.

"Ah, yes, the Grand, sir."

He delivered them and carried Lea's luggage inside. Slocum shouldered his saddle, and they entered the dimly lit, spacious lobby. A sleepy-eyed young clerk jumped to attention.

"Rudolph, sir, at your attention. What may I do for you?"

"Mrs. Howard and I wish a room. And two hot baths delivered to our room."

"Yes, of course, sir. I—I will arrange for that quickly."

"I trust you will." He set down his saddle and turned to her. "Lea, do you wish for any food service?"

She shook her head. "A bath and a clean bed will be sufficient."

"Very well then," Slocum said and signed in as Howard.

The clerk turned the register around and read the name. "Mr. Howard, we are pleased you have chosen our hotel. The tub and hot water will be up there in a few minutes. Room 225. It is on the front side. Is that satisfactory?"

He handed over the key.

"Don't be long on the tub arrangement. We have been on the train too long already."

"Yes, sir. I will have your bags and saddle delivered right up."

"Very good." He nodded to her and she led the way ahead of him up the wide staircase. The crystal chandelier gleamed, giving off sparkling lights like diamonds as they climbed the steps to the next floor and went down the hall to their room.

Slocum paused at the doorway before he inserted the key. "Your last chance to run me off."

"Not on your life," she whispered, and pushed his hand toward the keyhole. "I'd have put the bath off till morning if I'd been in charge."

"I still smell too much like a horse."

"It isn't my nose that needs some relief."

Inside the dark room, they were immediately in each other's arms and kissing. Her hungry mouth sought his like a drowning individual gasps for air. He soon discovered she was even taller than he had imagined. The rap at their door separated them.

A bellman delivered her two bags and a second man carried in his saddle and war bag. They moved apart and she took some pins out of her hair while Slocum dealt with the luggage. After both of the men had been tipped, four more people appeared with two copper tubs. A short woman in a white apron delivered several bath towels and at Lea's direction put them orderly-like on the bed.

"We will be right back, sir, with the hot water," the man in charge said.

When they filed out, he winked at her and shut the door. "They won't be long."

She looked at the dark ceiling for help and forced a smile in the lamplight. "I hope not."

At the sounds of people hurrying up the stairs, Slocum re-opened the door. It was some form of a brigade that brought the pails of steaming water through the door. The room soon smelled of hot water, and the lady in the apron gave Lea some soap and a long-handled brush. The man in charge ushered all the workers out. "Will that be all, sir?"

"Share this," Slocum said and handed him two dollars. He observed the rinse pails full on the floor and nodded. "Thanks."

He followed the man over and relocked the door. With his back to the door at last, he watched Lea undo the vest top, hang it on a ladder-back chair, then undo the blouse buttons. She paused and glanced up at him.

"Hey, you aren't undressing."

"I'm enjoying the view." His eyes still on her, he watched her lift the half slip over her head, and the long, pear-shaped breasts swung like firm weights. His boots toed off, he undid the gun belt and holster, the whole time watching her undo the denim skirt at the waist and step out of it. He looped his gun belt over the chair post, and she dropped her butt on the bed and began unhooking her shoelaces. The footgear soon off, she stood, hiked up her petticoats, and removed her silk stockings, carefully gathering them until, one at a time, they came off her toes.

By then he stood naked before her and she gasped at the sight of his rising sword. "Oh, I really chose well."

She quickly shed the slip and rose, with the vision of her precious breasts crossing his mind with wild headlines like "Rich Rancher's Wife Satisfies Horny Cowboy." They met in an embrace that ignited a fire in them like throwing coal oil on flames. Mouth to mouth, their naked skin pressed together, the intoxication of their mouths spread to their brains.

"The baths can wait," she gasped, and they fell upon the protesting bed. His fingers searched her pubic region and soon his thumb and forefinger began to rub her clit into action, making it arise into a stiff erection. Sprawled on her back, she cried out "Now, now!"

He moved between her raised, parted knees, realizing that she was lubricated enough for his entry. His nearly full erection slipped into her gates and she cried out with a sharp, "Oh!" as he passed through her tight ring. The bed beneath them began to whirl them away into a dazzling form of suspension, like being sucked down into a whirlpool. His efforts to connect with her became superhuman. Her interior began to spasm so hard that the pain shot to his brain again and again until he reached the bottom. Then the cannon fire from his gun rose in the base of his scrotum and, like a shot, exploded inside of her. They collapsed in a pile, and a dark curtain passed between them.

Somewhat recovered, he rose up on his arms to take some of his weight off of her, then he leaned over and whispered in her ear, "Again?"

She blinked her blue eyes in shock, then swallowed. "Hell, yes."

14

In midmorning while Lea was still asleep, Slocum tiptoed to the dresser and left a small penciled note: I WILL BE BACK.

Then he slipped out the door and went downstairs. He nodded to the clerk and went on out into the bright sunshine. With not a cloud in the sky, a soft southern breeze swept his face. There was plenty of traffic: wagon, buggies, Indian travois, freight haulers headed for the Dakota reservations. A man on a bicycle wobbling through the dried ruts just about collided with Slocum as he sought the far side of the street. He shook his head. Who in hell would use one of those things when there were plenty of good horses to ride?

The Red Lion Saloon's green batwing doors invited him. Maybe he could learn some word of Hudson's arrival in this busy berg. No way the man could have made it up here yet, but perhaps someone knew him or knew of some family or acquaintance he'd meet up here. Randle Hudson had some plans for this place—his brother Ulysses was too scared to lie about his destination when Slocum had secured him in the Vinita jail. However, Hudson could be aiming for Ogallala because of his knowledge of his sister's location, or it could be the place he'd met a dove he'd taken a fancy to sometime before. Or it could be he'd planned some underhanded thievery that posed an opportunity for him here. If Hudson stepped in Ogallala, Slocum would have a trap set and enough informers to let him know immediately what his location was.

The daytime bartender wasn't the man he'd met on his last pass through there. The new guy, Ernie, said, "Your friend who used to work here is in Nevada working in some gold strike boomtown."

"Ernie, that's fine. I'm looking for a killer. His name is Randle Hudson. He's headed here from the Indian Territory. May take him some time to get up here, but I'll pay a hundred bucks if you or anyone locates him when he arrives. He has a sister up here, Penelope Granger."

The barkeep shook his head. "Don't know her."

"Not a word to anyone, but I'll pay you thirty bucks if you can find her for me. That's all you've got to do, and if you have someone find him who claims the reward and says you sent him, I'll pay you thirty too."

Ernie set down the mug of beer in front of him. "Where will you be?"

"Right now at the Grand, but if I change sites, I'll tell you."

Ernie checked to be certain that no one could hear him before he spoke. "You've got a deal. I can ask around if anyone knows him. But if she's in town, I'll find her. Then I'll get word to you."

"Wonderful." Slocum nodded at him and sipped the ice cold beer. That was how beer was supposed to be served—ice cold. Two more bars, and his trap was set with the bartenders in both of them, the Texas Palace and Getner's Saloon. He went back to the hotel and removed his hat, coming quietly into their room.

Lea bolted up in bed, holding the sheet over her bare breasts. "Oh, my God, I thought you were gone forever."

"No, I left a note."

"Sorry, I didn't look for it."

"You want breakfast or lunch now?"

She swept the curls back from her face and let the sheet

drop, scooting over the bed to the edge. "No. I can eat anytime. What about you?"

He toed off his left boot. "I think you have other ideas."

"After last night's whirlwind, I want more of it."

"You know, you were hungry then, which made it keener than usual. The edge may be off of it today."

She ignored his words and was in his arms in a second. Their mouths meshed together, her hot tongue stirring him up. So they'd eat later. Her long, slender fingers pulled on his rod after he dropped his pants. As anxious as she was, he stomped them off his ankles, and they fell onto the bed with her trying to pull him up to her source. He closed his eyelids at the pleasure of his swift entry. Openmouthed, she gave a short cry and hunched her butt up to meet him. And so they coupled and uncoupled several times until they both lay on their backs, spent. In sheer exhaustion, they rolled back together and slept some more.

In the late afternoon when they were dressed, she looked anxiously out the window. "I'm going to miss the damn train, aren't I?"

"Probably."

She frowned and then shook her head as she drew back in. "And you don't give a damn, do you?"

He threw his legs off the bed, mopped his face in his callused palms, and shook his head. "I could stay here for a long, long time with you."

She looked at the ceiling for help. "You are no help for me at all, are you?"

"Not if you're leaving me."

She wagged a long finger at him. "I bet the minute I leave, you'll have a new woman in this bed before it gets cold."

"Me?"

"Don't play innocent with me."

In minutes, they were undressed and back on the mattress with springs squeaking underneath them. It was past five o'clock when they finally dressed and went out to eat. They were walking up the boardwalk toward a café a block away, where the desk clerk said they served great meals. He spotted three familiar riders coming down the street abreast and turned her toward a slot between two buildings to hide his face.

"Tell me where those three men on horseback are going."

"They've dismounted at the Red Lion. Who are they?"

"Three killers from the Indian Territory. One's named Rensler. He's the ringleader. The other two men I don't know."

"That's not who you want?"

"Oh, I want them, but I want Hudson worse."

"They're inside the Red Lion now and never even noticed you." She straightened like a proper woman and smiled. "You amaze me more and more every hour."

"Thanks. Let's go eat."

More things on his mind now with Rensler in town. He'd wire Hindman and ask for some assistance from the U.S. marshal's office there. Deep in his own thoughts of what to do next, he showed Lea inside the café.

They were seated in the restaurant and ordered coffee while they scanned the menu. Slocum was still uptight about Rensler being there.

When he laid down the menu, she reached across the table and squeezed his wrists. "You are such an intense person in everything you do. I have never met a person quite like you."

"Sorry if I am distracted now. I must tell you I have really enjoyed your company."

"I hope so. It has been very heady for me. But now there are two killers in your life to arrest, or remove from society anyway. What will you—"

The waiter returned and took their order. She ordered sliced roast beef, mashed potatoes, and farm fresh green beans. He ordered a large porterhouse steak and some potatoes. The waiter thanked them and promised to bring them back some fresh made coffee.

After he'd gone, they resumed their conversation. Slocum had searched the room twice by then and no familiar faces showed up. "So you left society in New York to be with your husband and his ranching project?"

"If I'd known he was going to haul me out here and stick me on some hilltop surrounded by sagebrush, I'd never have married him."

"I'm sorry."

"Don't be. My first husband, Leon Swartz, was killed at Gettysburg. He was a rather charming man, I thought at the time. But"—she surveyed the diners around them as if to be certain they didn't overhear her before she continued—"he was not a long-term lover. On our honeymoon, he usually became too excited and did not last long even if he didn't miss doing it before he was inside of me. I soon discovered maids did not excite him so quickly and he could rip them off.

"I thought the war might season him. Of course, he came home on furloughs twice, and I decided maybe he was seasoned enough—all I needed to do was wean him off the maids. Unfortunately, he was shot the first day of the battle." She shook her head, dismissing him.

"Two years later, I met Thomas at a polo match. He's older than I am by fifteen years. But he looked so stable and rich— he's an athletic man. So I played very demure and we had a very large wedding. On our wedding night, I discovered he was more concerned about his own physical condition than my body. Oh well. I soon fit well in his society and enjoyed it. I was Mrs. Thomas Malloy of Highland Estates. Opportunities exist in that society to suit my taste in other men since my husband was absent so much, either playing polo or worried about his ranch in Wyoming.

"And when I have the opportunity, I encourage him by telling him that he is such a lover, how could I want any more?" The waiter interrupted her with their food.

They ate their food, exchanging pleasantries. "I knew when you came to sit beside me on the coach that you were exactly what I needed. But I wondered then if I had the courage and looks to attract you."

"You had all the power."

She nearly blushed, and he winked at her between bites he'd cut off his large steak. Perhaps with needs like she had for sex, it was hard for her to find men with enough discretion to suit her. *My, my, what they had missed.*

"What shall you do about this second man, Rensler?" she asked.

"I think the U.S. marshal here can handle him. Several of Rensler's men are in the Fort Smith, Arkansas, jail awaiting trial on murder and rustling charges. There is a federal warrant sworn out for his arrest."

She nodded that she understood. "There is a train leaving for Cheyenne at nine tonight. We'd still have time to go—play. If you wanted to?"

"With a woman like you, my dear? Finish your meal. Where do you stay in Cheyenne? I'll be very discrete."

"I trust you. We have a residence there called Grand Manor. It sits on a ridge north of town. Thomas must have been a military commander in the war. He likes to be positioned on high places. Same as the New York residence. However, I understand he has it up for sale."

"So you will be stuck in Wyoming Territory?"

She gave him a peeved smile. "Yes."

After the meal they went back to the hotel and frolicked in the bed. She capped it off with a wild blow job on him and looked shocked when he came in her mouth.

Half gagging, she laughed and fought for her breath. "I thought your gun would be empty."

On the train platform, Slocum stood beside her as the black porter took her bags onto the train. They kissed and she let her arms drop slowly to her sides, then she shook her head. "I shall cry until you come to see me. Good luck, big man."

They parted and he watched the red lantern on the back railcar swinging off into the sunset in a curtain of coal smoke.

Oh well. Fashionable women like Lea were not easy to find in his world. Now, where was Penelope Granger? That would be his next move after he wired Hindman in Vinita about Rensler.

He went inside the train depot and wrote out a telegraph message for U.S. Marshal Hindman in Vinita, Indian Territory.

OUR MAN RENSLER IS IN OGALLALA, NEBRASKA. SAW HIM ON THE STREET TODAY. IF YOU HAVE A WARRANT FOR HIS ARREST, SEND IT TO THE LOCAL FEDERAL MARSHAL. I WILL TRY TO HELP HIM APPREHEND THE MAN.
SLOCUM

Slocum then left the office after paying the telegrapher.

At the hotel, he learned from the clerk that his "wife" had paid for another ten days' stay at the Grand for him and then he found two hundred dollars in paper money under his pillow. Where could he find Penelope Granger? He was unsure if she was a high-priced dove in a fancy house, a street hooker, or some tramp in the alley. So his quest began in the Texas Palace. There he got into a poker game and played cards. While he wasn't really playing as hard as usual, Lady Luck smiled on him and he won several large pots against two freighters, one who called himself Swain and another who gave his handle as Brock, and a Mr. Claude, who looked like a businessman but had already drunk too much to be engaged in competitive poker. The four men played cards with little conversation. Slocum had answered some of their questions about his business in town and then wondered aloud if any of them knew Penelope Granger. A cousin he was supposed to look up for his family.

"What she look like?" Brock asked, tossing in his hand.

"I have no idea," Slocum said. "You know about these look-up-family-members deals."

Brock chewed hard on his dry cigar and got ready to deal the next hand. "I'd bet there's twenty women by that name in these parts."

"I bet you're right," Slocum said. "Two more hands to beat me and I'm going to bed."

The players moaned that he had all their money and now he was going to leave them. He quipped, "That's simply how life goes."

When he left the Texas Palace, he sauntered up to the third saloon, Getner's. The place was fogged in tight with cigar smoke. And many of the men inside were coughing on it, standing three deep at the bar. He decided against entering the veiled saloon, went back to his room, and undressed—then lay awake on the bed for a couple of hours—it was no fun there without Lea.

Where in the hell could he find Penelope Granger? And what would he do about Rensler? He'd look up the local U.S. marshal in the morning. Finally he went to sleep, but it was not restful—he felt simply suspended between the real and almost, from which he awoke several times during the night finding he'd only had had his eyes shut for thirty minutes.

15

At dawn, Slocum was in a small café, crowded with unwashed workingmen gobbling down their food in a rush before they reported to work. The waitress swept a lock of blond hair from her face to take his order. Six feet tall, she looked like an Amazon woman he'd once seen in a historical book—only she wasn't bare breasted.

"What kin ah get'cha?" she asked.

"Ham good?" he asked.

"I guess. It ain't got any maggots in it."

"Good. Ham, fried eggs, biscuits, gravy, and black coffee."

"You're new here?" she drawled.

"Yes."

"Well, I'll turn this in for ya. It'll be come'n."

"Good, my first appointment isn't until noon."

"Hell, honey, I'll beat the dog shit out of that." Then she sashayed out to the kitchen, hollering his order at the cook. "Don't be long on it either."

On her way back, she brought the coffeepot and poured him a steaming mug. "What's your business in this place?"

"Cattle."

142

"Yeah, I see that by your Texas clothes."

Slocum nodded and noticed that most of the customers were fast leaving for their jobs. In minutes the place was near empty.

She soon came back by and checked on his coffee again. "I'll refill it. Your food is next. Married, single, or just act like it?"

"I guess I act like it. I have no wife."

"She die or you left her?"

"Never been married."

She gave him an I-don't-believe-that look, readjusted the lead pencil behind her ear, and shook her head, going after his food. "Ya tell a good tale anyway."

In a few moments she returned with his platter of food. "Anyway, tomorrow if you're still around, let that damn crowd get out of here and you'll get much better service."

"I'll remember that." He cut his eggs with the side of his fork and considered her.

She nodded. "That's number one. Two, I don't get off here until three this afternoon."

He lowered his voice. "I need to find a Penelope Granger."

With a questioning look on her face, she asked, "Would she be called Lupe?"

"All I know is her name."

"What's the deal?"

"I need to talk to her."

"I'll be off at three, like I said. Maybe we can find her."

"That's our secret, huh?"

She agreed and then grinned at him. "See you then."

He paid and tipped her good, then left to find the U.S. marshal's office. What was Rensler up to anyway? In the bright sunlight, he walked the wooden boardwalk and nodded to the ladies, both housewives and doves, who strode the same path. He asked a business suited man on the corner where the federal offices were located and was pointed toward the courthouse: a hastily thrown up two-story building still under construction with many rigs parked and horses tied around it. He could hear the handsaws as he smelled the fresh-cut wood.

"Marshal's office?" Slocum asked a young clerk amid the farmers and foreigners in the lobby.

"Second floor."

He thanked him and flowed with the crowd to the second floor. He went in the door marked U. S. Marshal. Slocum found himself away from the crowd when he entered the room. A man wearing glasses looked up from his desk. "Can I help you?"

"Who's in charge here?"

"Marshal Pense."

"May I talk to him?"

"He's downstairs in the courtroom. They are finishing construction on it. Can anyone else help you?"

"There is a wanted man in town who's responsible for the killing of several people down in the Indian Territory."

"What's his name?" The clerk looked bored by their conversation.

"Ralph Rensler."

The young man drew in his breath and then sighed in defeat. "There are several wanted men in this town. Why don't you have the local sheriff arrest him?"

Slocum reined in his anger and impatience. "I believe you have a request from the law down in the Indian Territory to arrest him."

"Hell, mister, we have a thousand requests a day for that around here."

"What is your business in this office?" Slocum looked around the room, bare of pictures or even a flag.

"You want an appointment or not?"

"I'll go find him." He turned on his heel and started to leave. He paused at the door. "I suppose I can tell all the people with federal warrants against them to enjoy their stay in Ogallala. The U.S. marshal's office doesn't give a damn."

Slocum never gave the boy a chance to answer his comments and closed the ill-fitting door behind himself. He found a balding man wearing a white shirt with his tie pulled loose talking to someone who was obviously a superintendent of construction about the jury box being built.

"The fence is too tall."

"Marshal, that's in the plan."

"Too tall. Cut it down six inches."

"That's not in the—"

"I don't give a damn. Cut it down six inches." A vein on the side of his face pulsed. He turned and looked mildly at Slocum. "What do you need?"

"A fugitive arrested."

"Who?'

"His name is Rensler. He's responsible for killing two of my men in the Indian Territory."

Pense nodded. "Who are you?"

"My name's Slocum."

Pense shook his head and extended his hand to shake with him. "I am undermanned here. I am patching what I can do. This courtroom has to be completed in two weeks. Wait— Deputy Marshal Joe Day is at home. I'll draw you a map to his place and you can find him. He'll arrest this guy, and we'll have one less fugitive in town."

"He's a tough guy."

"So is Joe. Turn it over to him." Pense found a paper and drew a map to the deputy's place. On the back he wrote for Joe to arrest this guy Rensler and that Slocum could identify him.

"Thanks," Slocum said.

"You must be sincere to have tracked him this far."

"I am."

Slocum found Joe Day nailing up the board fence on his milk cow's pen. Nails in his mouth, he nodded at Slocum's appearance, then went back to finish his nailing. That completed, he turned, took the remaining nails out of his mouth, and asked Slocum his business.

"Your boss wants you to arrest a fugitive who had two of my hands killed."

"Who's he?" He hung the hammer on the fence.

"Ralph Rensler."

"Where is he now?"

"Yesterday, he was in a saloon in town."

"He on the run?" Day recovered his brown coat from the fence. Looking over his workmanship, he said, "I hope that holds her."

Slocum nodded and introduced himself.

"Where do you think Rensler is at?"

"I saw him in town yesterday with two men I don't know. He was running a beef slaughter company in the Indian Territory."

"Let's go track him down."

"Fine." This man looked all business as they walked into his house and he told his wife what he was going to do. Slocum exchanged words with her, and then Slocum and Day hiked back to town. In the first saloon, Getner's, they found some card players in the dark interior. The bartender didn't recall anyone new who matched Slocum's description of a fortysomething big man in an expensive suit with two side-kicks. They left Getner's for the Texas Palace. The bartender in there, a man called Hal, said they'd been in there the day before and had stayed to themselves most of the time at a back table.

"They say where they were going or anything?" Day asked.

"Asked who was the cattle buyer for the Indian reservations in the north."

Day nodded. "You tell him?"

"Yeah, Ward Provisions Company, north of town."

"Across the river, isn't it?" Day asked.

"Yeah. Some senator from back East is supposed to own it. This guy acted like he knew the outfit. They left and I ain't seen them since."

Day nodded. "You think they went up there?"

The bartender nodded.

"It's a large operation across the river," Day told Slocum.

Deep in thought about Rensler's purpose, Slocum nodded,

unfamiliar with this outfit. They left the Texas Palace and Slocum fed the lawman lunch. They decided to ride out to the beef contractor in the morning.

Slocum parted with Day after the meal with plans to meet him at the livery at six A.M. to ride out to the operation and learn what they could about Rensler.

Three o'clock that afternoon, Slocum waited in the alley for the waitress from the café. She was talking a mile a minute to another unseen worker when she emerged from the back door of the café. Shocked to see him, she put on a pleased smile, then ran to hug him like a longtime friend. "Damn, I thought you'd—"

He kissed her and about had to stand on his toes to accomplish it. When they parted, she clutched his arm and looked at him, impressed. "You're real as hell. Wow, well, big man. Let's go talk to Granny Wren."

"Who's she?"

"Anyone lives in the shanty town in the Platte River willows, she knows them. If this Penelope is down here, Granny can tell us where she lives."

He observed how athletic this tall woman in her plain dress was as they strode down the dirt street, headed for the river. She definitely had muscles and acted like physical things were simply movable objects, demonstrated as she swept up a good-size stick and flung it at a barking dog. Slapped with the force of her throw, the cur left, yelping that he'd been hurt. Slocum smiled as she caught the crook of his arm again.

"I don't even know your name."

"Slocum."

"Hannah's mine. I had a husband once. He ran off with a much smaller woman that he could beat the hell out of."

"Where did you hail from?"

"Oh, hell, my family came out of Tennessee to Arkansas and then went to Kansas, but they hated us there 'cause we drawled. I ran off to marry this guy, who later left me. It was either become a whore or a waitress."

"No suitors?"

"None worth much. Who wants a woman whose feet hang over the end of the bed?"

He shook his head with no answer.

"That's Granny's place." She pointed it out.

A small ramshackle shack covered with tar paper stood in the head-high, swaying willows. The old lady seated in the rocker out front puffed on a clay pipe and nodded at their approach.

"Granny, this is Slocum. He's looking for a woman named Penelope Granger."

"Nice to meet'cha, sir. The name Penelope don't bring— oh, her name is Granger, huh?" The dried apple–wrinkled face shone at her internal discovery. "She lives over on Wood's Island."

Slocum frowned at Hannah.

"Oh, that's west of here."

"She is a nice woman with too many kids," Granny said, shaking her head. "Have a seat, my manners are so poor."

They drew up some wood kegs and nodded to her.

"You must be careful. I see trouble coming for you, sir." Granny beat the ashes out of her pipe in her wrinkled palm to be sure they started no fire.

Slocum nodded. "Are these men coming for me killers?"

She nodded. "Did they kill family or acquaintances?"

"One killed a friend in Texas. The other one had two of my hired cowboys executed."

"Be careful," she repeated and looked at him with grave concern.

"I need to go find these men. I appreciate your warning. Hannah has been working all day, and I imagine she's tired."

"Bless you two." Shakily, Granny rose and held out her arms to hug each of them.

He slipped twenty dollars into her apron pocket. She noticed, smiled, and shook her head. "You are way too generous."

"You deserve it. Thanks for your warning." He straightened and she looked wet eyed. "Bless you two."

Swinging on his arm, Hannah led him back toward town. "Satisfied?"

"Yes, you were a big help. I'd never have found Penelope Granger if you hadn't taken me to Granny. I am in your debt."

"Good, come to my place. I can fix some supper. You need to eat."

"All right."

"You're too easy to sway." She threw her head back to laugh aloud. "I am such an evil woman. My reputation is terrible and my plans for you for tonight would make a dove blush."

"One thing for certain. You don't need much coaching."

She looked around at the willows. "If the ground wasn't so damn sandy here, I might not wait."

"Oh, we'll make it back to your place," he assured her.

"Will you stay all night and hold me afterward?"

"I can."

"That's wonderful." She bent over in his face and kissed him hard on the mouth. They paused to savor the sweetness for a short while, then went on to her small house.

He found the one room a neat, clean, organized space with a table and a dry sink. Some blue china on the shelves, a few cast-iron skillets, and a Dutch oven. A small store of meal, oatmeal, and flour and lard all orderly in a row.

She stood before him and looked at the kitchen range, then at the patch quilt that covered bed. "What are you the most hungry for?"

He pushed off his boot with his toe and she laughed. Unbuttoning her dress down the front, she continued laughing, almost beside herself. "I am too."

In minutes, naked, she turned back the covers. Undressed, he admired her snowy body, and when his palm ran over her back, she swallowed hard and straightened.

"No rush," he said to settle her.

"Good, I really am pleased—"

His mouth silenced her. His chest full of her large pear-shaped breasts and the hunger in her efforts all told him he had lots to enjoy. They soon fell into the surf of her sheets and waves of pleasure swept over them. The calmness soon became a deep desire that drowned them in a fire of passion and physical strength.

My God, what a woman. . . .

16

A cool morning wind swept his freshly shaven cheeks as Slocum saddled the livery horse in the lamplight. He was pleased that Hannah had to be at work so early. It gave him time to have an early breakfast before renting a pony and being ready for Joe Day when he rode up.

"You must be an early riser," Day said when they met.

"I can get around early, though I am used to a camp cook's bell ringing."

"I checked a little more at the office yesterday. Those men riding with Rensler may be wanted too. I have five warrants from Marshal Hindman in Vinita for five other men who may be connected to him."

"Good, we can clean up the whole gang," Slocum said. "If we can find them."

"I thought the same thing. I wonder if they're out at this Ward Provisions Company. I have never been to their operation. I understand it is quite extensive. They gather large herds of beef there to drive to the reservations."

"Someone said an Eastern state senator owned the firm."

Day nodded as they crossed the new long bridge across the sluggish Platte River. "I don't know his name either. Why?"

"Rensler was in the beef procurement business for the railroad that they are building across the northern tier of the Indian Territory. You reckon there's a connection?"

Day simply nodded. "We may find out."

The Ward Provisions Company operation was expansive, as Slocum and Day found when they reached the vast corrals, barns, hay operation, and buildings. All painted bright red, they were impressive. The two men dismounted in front of a building marked General Offices and hitched their horses, and Day led the way to the French doors.

Once inside they removed their hats. A balding man wearing square-cut glasses came into the room and frowned at them.

"May I help you?"

"U.S. Deputy Marshal Joseph Day, sir. This is my posse man, Slocum. We are looking for a Ralph Rensler."

"On what sort of business?"

"I have a warrant for his arrest from the federal court in Fort Smith, Arkansas, for murder and rustling."

"I am sorry. There is no such Ralph Rensler here."

Day's back rose with indignation at the man's words— "no such here." "I have the authority of the federal court to examine your books, sir. Rensler works either for you or for a subsidiary of this firm. Now, where is he?"

"You will have to speak to our lawyers in Washington, D.C."

"Listen, I'm not messing with no far-off lawyers. That man is here." Day pointed at the polished hardwood floors.

"Sir, I will have to send for my security if the two of you don't leave immediately."

"You won't dare shoot a federal marshal or his posse man. Now, where in this place is our man?"

"You have no authority—"

"Slocum, search the house." Day gave him a head toss.

Slocum agreed and went through the room full of wide-eyed accountants and on into the back rooms stacked with boxes. No one there.

"Where do the men sleep?" he asked a young man seated at a desk, who looked worried.

"Bunkhouse." He pointed across the manicured lawn to a building near the barns.

"Thanks." Slocum went back up front and told Day that if they were on the place, they might be at the bunkhouse across the lawn.

"We'll go there next. His name is Pritchard," Day said indicating the stubborn man they had met first. "You too, Pritchard. You go ahead. If they shoot at us, they'll get you first on this deal."

"You have no authority to do this. You will lose your jobs over this matter." His voice rose a little higher with each threat. "I will have you fired!"

"Keep walking—"

Slocum grabbed Day's arm and jerked him back at the tinkling of breaking glass. "There's someone got us in their sights."

The two of them made it to the side of the office unscathed. Someone in the second story of the bunkhouse was shooting a rifle at them. The smoke of the shots was boiling out of the window. Pritchard was running the other way and screaming, "Don't shoot, for God's sake!"

The man tripped and fell facedown in the grass. Slocum and Day emptied their pistols at the window and then crawled back to safety to reload. Pritchard's crying could be heard from where Slocum, along with Day, sat on his butt. *What in the hell is he crying for? He isn't even shot.* Guns ready, Slocum and Day rose and ran for the barn.

There were enough bushy evergreen trees to give them some cover. They slid one of the double doors open, and the wine smell of stabled horses reached Slocum's nose. Running to the other end, they found a walkway through a door on the west side at the back. Plenty of fine-smelling hay in the tall stack, Slocum decided, looking around the shadowy barn's interior for signs of anyone.

Then he heard the sounds of horse riders and hooves

drumming the ground. Day looked over at him, shocked. "They must be getting away."

They crossed the grounds in time to see two fleeing riders cross it, whipping their horses to escape. Slocum ran inside the bunkhouse and looked at the open staircase, satisfied that the shooter might still be up there. His loaded six-gun in his fist, he eased his boot sole on the whipsawed pine step. It only gave a small creak, and Slocum made a "be silent" sound to Day as the marshal burst through the open door.

"Hell, I don't see anyone in here. Let's go get our horses," Day said, to make the suspect upstairs think they were leaving.

"Sure," Slocum agreed, easing up the staircase.

"Let's go," Day said and slammed the door shut, remaining inside. Slocum advanced silently toward the second floor landing. He thought he heard the scuffle of feet coming toward him, and he paused, pointing the pistol's muzzle at the opening. His heart thudded under his breastbone and he listened so hard his ears hurt.

Then a cough told him the shooter was about halfway between the north window and the exit stairs. Slocum would have to charge him when he drew much closer. He removed his hat and set it on the step. Then, after he gathered himself up, he charged up the stairs and looked down the room to where the gunman sat on his butt, holding his bleeding leg.

"I'm shot."

Slocum took the man's gun away from him and shook his head. "I really don't feel sorry for you. Where did Rensler go?"

When the man didn't answer, Slocum kicked him hard in the side with his boot toe. "Where is he going?"

"Damn, you busted a rib." He bowed over, holding his side. "I'm shot and bleeding to death on the floor."

"Yeah, you'd've done worse than that to me if you had the upper hand. Where's Rensler going?"

"I guess out of the country. He never told me."

"I'm not a patient man and I'm not above cutting off your ear."

"All right, all right. Cheyenne."

"Who will hide him out there?"

At the sight of Slocum's hunting knife, he put up his hands. "I don't— No, no, I'll tell you. There's a railroad headed north from there."

"It must be close to Douglas by now, huh?"

"I need a doctor. I don't want to die."

"What's your name?" Day was squatting down on the floor.

"Casey McDonald."

"Good," Day said, nodding his head. "I've got a Fort Smith warrant for him. At least we'll get paid for today," he said to Slocum.

Slocum holstered his knife. "We want all their things. They won't need them."

When he turned he saw three men wearing some private badges with rifles standing on the steps. Their leader demanded, "Who in the hell are you two?"

"U.S. Deputy Marshal Joe Day and my posse man, Slocum."

The older of the men frowned. "What are you doing on this property?"

"Looking for who's harboring criminals on their property. Two got away. You want to face those charges?"

"Hell no."

"Then get this man to Ogallala and the doctor. Then I may not consider your part in this a crime, as I do now. Well, don't stand there. Get him to the doc!" Day shouted at the men.

Slocum and Day went through the men's war bags for any evidence. They did find some letters from Ward Provisions addressed to Ralph Rensler. At last, Slocum and Day were ready to go back to Ogallala. The wounded man they'd had hauled off to town would be there when they got there.

"How's it all tied to the senator?" Day asked as they rode back in the midafternoon.

"Damned if I know, but we do know Ward Provisions has some hand in these beef contracts."

"Shit fire, there ought to be a way to lock them all up for doing it."

"Hell, Joe, nothing is that easy."

"Guess you're right. What're you doing in the morning?" Day asked.

"Going after a woman whose brother murdered a good man down in Texas."

"Where's she at?"

"Wood's Island."

"Who's she?"

"I don't care about her. I want her brother, who's on his way up here to stay with her."

"I'll ride along. I want to see how you handle a damn woman." Joe laughed.

Slocum went by the livery and paid for another day's rent on the horse. He went by the butcher shop, stood in line with some housewives, and picked up some beef, then rode over to Hannah's cabin and unsaddled his pony. She must have heard him because she came running around the corner of the house. A high-pitched scream in her throat, she about took him down tackling him.

"You came back. Oh, Slocum, I never expected to see you again. I was afraid I wasn't handy enough to suit you." Kissing him, she looked taken aback and surprised when he handed her the wrapped package of steak he'd bought for them.

"Silly. Why, you're handy enough for any man." He flat-handedly spanked her on the rump, and she straightened while trying to unwrap the package.

"Well, good." She gave up short of opening it, and they headed through the cabin door with his arm on her shoulder.

"I bought us some fresh cut steaks in that package."

"That may be better. Then my bacon and eggs idea won't be needed. Tell me about today." She led him inside.

"We have one of Rensler's men, Casey McDonald, in jail. He was shot in the leg but his boss and another man got away. They fled the place fast, and I told Joe Day we'd look for him later."

"I don't know McDonald. And tomorrow?" She set the meat package on her dry sink and undid the bindings, then approved of his purchase with a nod.

"We'll see if we can learn if Rensler really fled the country and then check on the Hudson brothers' sister."

"Penelope, huh?"

He nodded. Before he sat on the straight-backed chair, he took off his hat and put it on a wall peg. "I figured some suitor might be here by the time I got back and I'd have to cook them on a stick for myself."

She laughed, peeling potatoes, and shook her head. "I told you once. Who wants a woman whose big feet hang over the end of the bed?"

"I don't mind."

She put down the potato in her hand, then came over and kissed him on the cheek. "You sure know how to flatter a woman. But I'm too tall. I scare most men away."

"It's a damn shame."

"Well," she said, going back to her peeling and looking at the underside of the cedar shake roof, "I could do this food fixing later and nothing would rot. You dying hungry?"

He grinned at her. "For what?"

"Damn, why didn't you say so when you came?" The peeled whole spud dropped into the cold water, and she quickly dried her hand. "This is going to be lots better than food."

"Yes." He rose and began to toe off his boots. She was undoing her dress. He hung his gun belt on the chair's post, admiring her long legs as she took the slip off over her head,

In seconds they were kissing. Mouth to mouth they about fell on the bed, magnetized tightly to each other. He let her loose to sit on the bed, and she scrambled to the far side to sit up and hugged her legs in the shadowy light of the room.

He put his knee on the bed and she lay down. When he kissed her large dark nipples, she shuddered as if cold and wrapped her long arms around his body to pull him down on top of her.

"I like a man who knows what he wants." She spread her legs apart and nodded for him to go ahead. He felt for her clit and kissed her. In response to his teasing and kissing, she wiggled some and then began to cry.

"Am I hurting you?"

"No. No. I'm just so happy you came back. I'm fine—" She sobbed, clutching him tight as he inserted his rising erection through her gates. With a gasp, she arched her neck and head back and raised her butt up for more of him. Then with a soft, "Yes," she settled into helping him forget the whole damn day.

17

The steaks tasted good, much later under the lamplight. Since Hannah was wearing nothing but a wash-worn robe, Slocum could look across the table and see her deep cleavage. She smiled lots in between bites of food.

"I'm still here," she said and shook her curly blond hair as if she didn't believe all this was happening.

"Don't fly away," he teased.

"Now, Slocum, I ain't going to leave you, my friend. You're too damn much fun. If I thought half my customers would be as great in bed as you are, I'd haul my butt up to Miss Criscoe's Parlor house and start work up there."

"I don't figure you were cut out to be a lady of the night. You have a nice garden out back, raise lots of things, keep a nice tidy house. There is a right guy somewhere on this earth that would give his eyeteeth to have you in his bed, feet and all."

"But where?"

"How about looking for him at a church?"

"I ain't never tried that." She looked taken aback. "I figured they'd shun me, and I never dared go in one since I was a little girl."

"Find one where you feel comfortable. Church women can't stand for nice women to live alone."

"Me, nice?"

"You don't chew. You don't drink. I think you way under-sell yourself."

"My knees are weak just dreading it."

"Just be a little hard to get." He'd looked at the piece of steak on his fork. "Men like that."

"I may make a damn fool of myself."

He shook his head. "I've never seen you do that."

"You don't know me."

"Inside or out?"

Her face turned red. "I mean I can be a real bitch."

He shrugged. "Don't let it ruin your life or the one you're building on."

"If I do all this—what will I find?"

He picked up his coffee cup and paused. "A person good enough to share his life with you."

"Are you interested? I mean in me."

"I'm a man on the run. My past chases me. I can't remain long in one place."

She closed her eyes and nodded. "I figured so. But I'd take you."

"I'm no bargain. I'll have to head west in a short while. Rensler's man said earlier his boss would head for Cheyenne next. So after I find Hudson, I'll need to go out there, I guess."

She put down her fork, rose, and leaned over the table. He put down his cup, rose up and over enough, and kissed her on the mouth.

Then she went for more coffee. "Well, you sure make me believe I'm someone." She wet her lips. "I can't hardly be-lieve it will work."

They spent the night in each other's arms and she woke sometime in the early morning. Kissed him good-bye and said for him to come by the café for breakfast before he left. He went back to sleep and still woke up before the sun came up. He took a sponge bath, shaved, and saddled his horse. He had forgotten what time he was supposed to meet Joe Day. Hell, no matter, he'd still be there at the livery early enough.

After his breakfast, Hannah went out into the alley and kissed him good-bye. "You be careful. That island is a kinda tough place where some outlaws hang out."

"Hell, I'm riding with the federal law out there."

"They shoot them too."

He laughed and spanked her as she stepped away. "I should be back tonight."

"I'll fix something that will hold until then."

He swung on the bay horse and headed for the livery. Day should be there to meet him by this time.

The lawman had not made it yet when Slocum arrived, so he hitched his horse and sat on the bench out in front to wait on him. Main Street began to blossom with traffic. Freight wagons, delivery wagons, a well-dressed man drove up to the livery in a doctor's rig and left his horse to be put up.

"That the other doc here?" Slocum asked the swamper who was unhitching the horse.

"Naw, he's the banker. Alfred Newton the Third." Then he took the light-footed horse to put him away inside.

Joe arrived and they rode out together for the road west.

"You get some sleep last night?" Joe asked.

"Some."

"I couldn't hardly sleep. Thinking about that damn Rensler's man McDonald shooting at us and Rensler running away."

"Rensler takes good care of himself," Slocum said. "I think he worked for that Ward bunch when he was running that deal down in the Territory, and they never expected us to come looking for him out here."

"They'd do to be investigated some, even if a U. S. senator does own them," Joe said. "That Pritchard, telling me he'd have my job is a threat. I may be the one who has his job when it's all over."

"I hope we find his sister today and learn all she knows about Randle Hudson and his plans."

"You going on to look for Rensler out west after that?"

"He had two good men executed who discovered his butcher camp and tried to stop him. They were both shot in the back of the head. Another cowboy and I found their grave and dug them up. He don't deserve any mercy in my book. Like this Randle Hudson and his brother, who is in a Texas jail by now. They were riffraff floated down into Texas. Had avoided Parker's men for several years. They shot my friend for a few dollars in a robbery-murder and left like scalded dogs."

"I can say one thing after yesterday—I'd ride with you to the ends of the earth. You need to stay here and we can team up. Why, the two of us could round up enough wanted guys to make a good living."

"Thanks for your confidence. I hope we get word about Randle this morning. I never knew they even had a sister until I arrested Ulysses down in the Territory. When I got that news I headed up here. You know the rest."

"You think about staying around. We'd make a good team."

"Your cow stay in?"

"Oh, damn, I hope so. Or my wife will be hard to live with."

They both laughed.

The rickety long wooden bridge across the Platte River to the Wood's Island made Slocum wonder if it might collapse under a heavy load. The tall trees on the island had escaped the tongue of prairie fires over the years. Several had been cut down but still some huge trees towered over them.

Slocum stopped a woman wrapped in a blanket coming down the road. Though not Indian, her hair was matted and her face unwashed.

"Ma'am?" he asked, "You know Penelope Granger?"

With her front teeth missing, she grinned big. "You want me?"

Then she opened the blanket and exposed herself from her

flat, shrunken breasts to her black-haired crotch. "Me better than her."

"No, ma'am. I'll find her." He checked the bay horse and Day began to laugh.

"She wants you."

"Sorry, she ain't getting me either," Slocum said. "Let's ride. She ain't all there."

Once free of the crazy woman and down the sandy ruts a ways, Day shook his head at Slocum. "She's nuts."

There were some painted Indian tepees with small, dark-eyed Indian children wearing only tops playing around them.

"You can tell what they are anyway," Day pointed out to him.

"Indians don't worry much about clothes." Slocum was twisting in the saddle, looking around for a white residence. He spotted some smoke coming from a campfire and saw a canvas fly stretched for a shade between some trees.

A woman bent over tending a fire straightened up, and Slocum saw that she was pregnant. Her large belly tented out her dress in front. He rode over, dismounted, and took off his hat to approach her.

"Penelope Granger?"

"Yes." She blinked at what he wanted from her.

"My name is Slocum." He didn't want her to know Ulysses was in jail. "Are your brothers here?"

"No." She shook her head. "They ain't in Nebraska. Last I heard from them, they were working on a railroad down in the Territory."

"Penelope—"

She corrected him and nodded to Day. "They call me Lupe."

"You know a few weeks ago they shot and robbed a man down in Texas?"

Her dark eyes looked at him suspiciously. "They said they was in a shooting scrap with a man down there who tried to steal one of their horses. Said they caught him red-handed."

"I'm sorry, but they robbed and shot a family man for a few dollars."

With a frown of disbelief, she shook her head. "Well, they sure ain't here. You can see that—"

She ran over and swept up a baby still in diapers away from her cooking pots. "You can't touch them, dear. You'll get burned." Holding him in front of her large belly she shook her head. "I can't help you."

"Tell him if he comes here, he better give himself up." Day said.

"Won't do no good," she said, about ready to cry.

"Anything we can do for you, ma'am?" Slocum asked.

"Yes, get this kicking mule inside my belly out of me." She set the baby down and wiped the tears away.

He tipped his hat and they rode off.

"You still reckon he's coming here?" Day asked once they were out of her hearing.

"Hell, yes, and we found her. But I doubt he was here today or she'd've been more nervous."

Day agreed and they headed back to Ogallala. Another day wasted, but Slocum had located Hudson's sister and seen the conditions she lived under. Made a man wonder how some folks got by.

He and Day parted at the livery. The lawman shook his hand. "Any way I can help, you let me know." Then he rode off.

Slocum rented his horse for another day, cancelled his room, and collected the refund at the hotel—finally, after recalling how Lea had paid it up. Then with his war bag from the room, he rode out to Hannah's place. He could put his horse, Bay, on a long tether. There was plenty of grass there.

He found Hannah hoeing in her garden in the late afternoon. Busy cutting off small weeds growing in her rich black soil with the hoe, she looked well qualified to handle it. She paused and leaned on the handle.

"I thought you'd be late getting back. Was he down there?"

"I don't think so. The sister is powerful pregnant and

looked uncomfortable, busy cooking. Of course they told her they simply had a gunfight in Texas."

"Well, let's go see if my stew is worth anything."

"I'll tie Bay up and join you shortly."

"I'm just proud you came by one more time. I feel so relaxed with you, I can't even explain it. Serenity. Is that the word? You don't put any pressure on me and I can't hardly wait till you get back here."

He undid the girth and took the saddle and blanket off the gelding. She stepped in and kissed him. "I was going to be all cleaned up when you got back here—late."

"Now I'm early."

"We can talk later. See you at the house." She winked mischievously at him and went off whistling "Sweet Betsy from Pike."

With his horse tied out, he packed his gear to Hannah's front porch. He could see her sponging off in the kitchen corner. Her white skin shone in the shafts of light coming in through the four-pane window. Lots of woman standing there. When he stepped inside, she turned demurely away from him.

"See, I am used to being alone here. No shame, I guess."

"The scenery is nice." He drank some water from a dipper on the water pail.

"Plenty of it anyway."

"There you go again. You are a pretty, well-proportioned woman."

"Good. I'll tell myself that more often."

"It might help. Wait, I hear a horse coming. I'll go outside and see who it is, and you can get dressed."

"Yes," she agreed and he went out the door, closing it behind himself.

It was Day who rode up on his hard-breathing horse. "Like to never found you. Her husband, Granger, came and looked me up an hour or so ago. He asked to split the reward on your man, Hudson."

"He out there?"

"All he asked was for him to get half the reward if he showed us where he was at."

"Fine with me." Slocum heard the door open behind his back.

"Hannah, this is Marshal Day, the man I told you about."

"Good day, sir."

"Same to you, ma'am. Granger acts like Hudson might flee anytime."

"That's fine with me. Where do we meet him at?"

"At the small store above the island."

"I better get my horse. Hannah—"

"I heard enough. Go get him. Supper can wait."

"I may be real late."

She dismissed his concern. "No problem. You be careful."

He shouldered his saddle and headed for the bay. This might be the chance he needed to have Randle Hudson arrested or buried. The pad and saddle on his horse, he drew up the girths. Hannah stepped in and kissed him hard, then stepped back.

She looked hard at the ground. "Don't get hurt. I'm going to pray for you."

"Cheer up. He's not that tough an outlaw."

"I can still worry about you."

"Thanks." He swung into the saddle and nodded to her. Then he followed Day, who started off. The trip up there would take a few hours and it would be dark by then. No matter, Day had taken lots of trouble to find Slocum about this matter. His extra effort impressed him as they trotted their horses.

"How did you find me?" Slocum asked, riding beside him.

Day shook his head. "It wasn't easy. But I have my sources."

Slocum laughed. "Sorry, I didn't feel like it was necessary to tell you where I was at."

"I didn't intend to let this guy get away from you."

Slocum nodded and thanked him.

The sun was setting and the last half hour of glaring

bloody light was shining on the shack of a store. Day nodded to Slocum as they approached the slab-sided structure.

"Maybe we can get something to eat inside," Slocum offered.

"If it isn't in a can, don't eat it." The man shook his head.

"How about peaches?"

"Fine. The couple who runs it is sure not clean. That's Granger with his horse." Slocum saw a horse out by some pens and someone under a floppy brimmed hat that looked to be in bad shape.

"About time you got up here," the unshaven man said.

"I told you I had to find Slocum," Day said, stepping down.

The man in his thirties, dressed in filthy clothes, stuck out his hand. "You bring the money?"

"When we have him, we'll pay you." Day looked over at Slocum for his consent.

Slocum nodded. "Is Hudson at your place?"

"I risked my gawdamn life even coming here. Pay me."

"Listen, Granger, I'm not paying a damn thing until you show me Hudson."

"He'll kill me in a minute if he knows I'm snitching on him."

"Where's he at?" Slocum ignored the man's whining.

"When do I get my reward?"

"When you show us where he is. I'm not paying nothing until I see him."

"How do I know you'll pay me?"

"Daylight's about gone." Day said. "Tell us or the deal's off."

"All right, all right. He's staying in a camp on the west end of the island."

"Who's with him?" Day demanded.

"A breed and some fuzzy-faced kid."

"Draw us a map in the dirt," Slocum said, concerned about the dimming light.

"Cross the bridge, turn right. Their camp is at the west end of the island."

Looking around their surroundings to be certain they were alone, Slocum asked him, "How will we know it's his?"

"He's the only one at the end of the trail."

Still unsure about their informer, he turned to Day. "Let's ride."

"Don't tell him I sent you."

Slocum shook his head and mounted his horse.

"You owe me," he said after them.

Neither man said another word. They crossed the rickety bridge, which sounded hollow under their horses' hooves. Slocum wondered if this was his final time to have to trap Hudson. All this based on the scruffy Granger's word—a person he wouldn't trust in most cases as being completely truthful.

The twilight soon sank to near darkness. Not familiar with the area, they rode slow on the winding trail through the willows and under the canopy. At last they dismounted and went on foot. Day carried a sawed-off shotgun.

On the gentle night wind Slocum could smell cottonwood smoke. The particular scent had a wine to it he knew well and disliked. They hitched their horses and with stealth crept up on the camp.

"He'll run if he gets the chance," Slocum warned Day.

The lawman nodded and held the short shotgun barrel up.

Slocum listened to the faint conversation. Then someone said, *"Randle."*

With a satisfied nod, they stepped up, and Slocum could make out three figures sitting in the orange firelight. No doubt they sat waiting for something to cook, their interest centered on a carcass on a crude spit.

"What is it?" Randle jumped up.

"Hands high or die." Slocum stepped out of cover with his pistol held in his fist at eye level.

"I give up!" Hudson screamed.

"Don't—" Day leveled the shotgun at the shorter one, who tried to scramble to his feet and draw. The orange fire muzzle of the shotgun blast cut him down and some pellets must have hit the other two, for they both fell over.

"I gave up—" Hudson was twisting in pain on his back. "I'm hit."

Slocum stepped in and disarmed him. "Your man should have minded us."

Some of Day's buckshot had struck the breed in the side of the head; he wouldn't be moving on his own ever again. Slocum knelt down beside the lawman and clapped him on the shoulder. "You had no choice. You watch Hudson. I'm going to saddle some horses."

"What were they cooking?" Day asked. "I ain't eaten in a while."

"Check it out. I'll gather the horses."

Day agreed and Slocum went for their horses. Several curious residents had begun to gather.

"What's going on?" one old man asked.

"U.S. Marshal Day arresting some fugitives. Two of them are dead."

"Hmm, you guys always shoot them?"

"No. They made their own choice to fight us." Slocum brought their horses back to camp. He noticed Hudson was sitting up. Some woman he didn't know was cutting up the wild turkey taken from the spit.

"It's burned on one side," she said, looking up at him.

"It don't matter," Slocum said, satisfied that his long quest to find Rip Wright's killers was over. Hudson would live for the trial and walk to the top of the Texas scaffold with his brother. That wouldn't help Wright's widow except that she'd know justice had been served. Chewing on the slab of turkey breast meat that the woman handed him, Slocum's mouth twisted at the hated taste of the cottonwood smoke flavor. But along with the bitter burned taste, it would have to do. They were hours away from Hannah's.

Slocum and Day rode way into the night, delivering the two corpses and Hudson to the jail, where a doctor was called in to treat the wounded outlaw. When Slocum shook hands with Day as he was about to leave, he thanked the man again. "I guess that Granger will find you first."

Slocum dug out his roll and peeled off the money to give to Day.

"I imagine he'll be around to collect it," Day said. "Where can I send your share?"

"You keep it. I owe you that much."

"You don't owe me anything. I owe you." Day shook his head. "Where're you going next?"

"Cheyenne. I have one more thing to settle: Rensler, if I can find him."

"I figured so."

"I'm tired enough to sleep for two days."

"Not a bad idea. If you ever need help, call on me."

"Thanks. You're a tough partner in this business."

They parted at the jail and Slocum rode Bay back to Hannah's under the stars. Out on the prairie somewhere a coyote yapped away. He smiled to himself. *Keep talking. I'm listening, you old clown.*

18

Hannah had already gone to work—how he'd missed her Slocum didn't know. He undressed and fell on the bed. Out of a fuzzy world, he was awakened by an excited Hannah, who was jumping on top of him in the bed. When he met her eyes, she began kissing him and they were soon making serious business out of it. She managed to shed her skirt and drawers. With her slip raised up to her waist, he crowded in to couple with her. His breathing had grown faster. He furiously headed for some deep pleasure, his hands gripping the cheeks of her rump to go as deep as he could. She urged him on with her arms wrapped around him.

Then he felt two hot needles in his ass and he drove to the bottom of her well. The cannon roared and she clutched him tight. Slow-like she melted away and threw her arms out in complete surrender.

"Damn, I heard at work that you got him. They said several were shot, but someone finally told me you and Day were all right." She closed her eyes. "Thank God."

"Hudson will live to stand trial."

"And you're leaving." She rose and quickly shed the rest of her clothing. Standing hugging her treasures, she looked down at him. "I've never been that excited ever before in my life."

He stood up and took her in his arms. "It was sweet."

With her in his arms and her firm nipples in his chest, he rocked her back and forth. "Any man worth his salt in this world would never let you go. I promise you. You deserve him too."

"That means you're leaving me." She looked ready to cry.

"There are lots of things in my life that happened in the past that I can't control or straighten out."

"When will you leave?"

"The first train west."

She kissed him. "Then my time is short."

He agreed, then she pushed him down on the bed. "You still have lots to do."

Slocum climbed into the passenger car and headed for Cheyenne in the dark, his saddle and war bag stored in the stove space. He found an empty seat in the dim light. His fourteen-hour trek started with the jerk of the cars. In front of the depot he could see Hannah's tall figure waving at him. He returned it and was gone in the night. Settled down, he dozed and awoke when the sunlight filtered into the car. His mouth dry and his eyes slow to focus, he blinked and then looked around the car clacking on the rail joints.

Most of his companions were asleep. When the train reached the depot, he departed with his saddle and war bag. He took a taxi to the Drover's Hotel and checked in. He'd need a horse and knew Sam Houston at the Foot Hills Livery would find him a good one. No kin to the former Texas leader, Sam was a longtime friend of Slocum's. The liveryman might even know if Rensler was still about town or had gone north.

Slocum found lunch in a small café. Grateful for the fresh coffee, he ate the sliced roast beef, mashed potatoes, and green beans with sourdough bread on the side.

Then he went down the block to the Trail's End Saloon and

ordered a beer at the bar. Looking over the morning crowd, he saw no familiar faces. He paid for the beer and went over to the poker game in the back. Some likely looking sweat-stained hats in the circle told him they might be drovers and not professional gamblers.

The players saw him looking on and one invited him to get in. He declined and thanked them. He doubted there were any answers in the game that would serve his needs, deciding instead that he better find Sam. The beer finished, he put the stein on the bar and headed for the batwing doors. Stopped between the swinging doors, he noticed Lea driving by in a light buggy.

He sprinted across the porch and called to her. She reined in the horse and turned with a startled look in her eyes.

"Sorry to bother you, ma'am," he said, with his hat in hand. "But I wondered if you knew—"

"Oh, yes," and she lowered her voice. "Where can we meet?"

"Name it."

"Where do you stay?"

"Drover's Hotel."

"I'll send you a note."

"Yes, ma'am, I would appreciate that."

She winked at him and drove on. Obviously she felt exposed stopping and talking to a stranger on the street. He replaced his hat and acted like it all was casual. Back on the boardwalk, he recalled their short time together. Not bad. He headed for the livery.

He found his friend with his dusty boots resting on the rolltop desk. Sam blinked twice and threw his feet down.

"I swear it is you, Slocum." He shoved his hand forward to shake, then hugged him. "What are you up to?"

"Looking for a killer." Then Slocum told him all about Rensler and the execution of the two cowboys.

"I haven't heard of him. Where might he be?"

"If not here, he may be with the rail building going north. He has some ties to the company supplying beef to the crew."

Sam showed him a chair. "That belongs to some politician back East."

"A U.S. marshal in Nebraska said the same thing."

"You have any grounds to go after him?"

"Yes. There's a federal murder warrant from the federal court in Fort Smith, Arkansas, out for him."

Sam whistled. "That's Judge Parker's court."

"Yes, they already have several of his men in the jail."

"How did he get away?" Sam gripped his legs and leaned in to hear Slocum's answer.

"He has contacts and money to carry him out of the grasp of the law."

"What can I do for you?"

"I need to buy a horse and get up there and look for him."

"Hell, take whatever one you want."

"I can afford—"

"Is anyone taking up your expenses out here?"

"No."

"Then I'll help you. Pick out a horse and I'll see what I can learn about this guy."

"Thanks for your help, Sam. I'll let you check around and stay around town a few days until we get a better handle on his location."

Sam agreed and they shook hands. After thanking his friend again, Slocum walked back to the Trail's End Saloon and joined the poker game. Freighters, cattle drive bosses, and a hardware storekeeper sat around tossing in money on bets or hands that had no value. Slocum won and lost, met the players, and the day rolled on. When he quit he found he had earned fifty dollars and had made some friendships with a few who might help him on his quest. John Doolin, whose teams and wagons freighted north past the rail's invasion. Also Cory Thomas, who ran a lumber yard–hardware store.

Doolin walked him outside in late afternoon. "You never said your business, but you look like a man on a mission to me."

Slocum stepped away from the doorway. "I'm looking for

a killer who had two of my employees murdered in the Indian Territory. He had those men executed by shooting them in the back of the head."

"What's his name?"

Slocum looked over the traffic passing by. "His name is Ralph Rensler, and he has connections with the Ward Provisions Company supplying the railroad contractor."

The man smiled. "If he's up there, my men will find him. We're hauling the food goods up there twice a week."

"Ralph Rensler. Watch him, he's a back shooter."

"If he's up there, I'll have them wire me."

"If I'm not here, you can give Sam Houston at the livery the message. I trust him and he can get me the word."

"I can do that. Good luck," Doolin said, his blue eyes set and determined.

Slocum thanked him and wondered if by this time Lea had sent him a message. No telling. He checked the desk at the Drover's and the desk clerk handed him an envelope. He took it outside and then opened the sealed message.

> *Dear Slocum,*
>
> *There is a cabin on the ranch near here. No one uses it anymore. I can meet you there after lunch tomorrow. The map is on the back. He is working on the house up at Douglas and I don't expect him to return for a week. My marital situation here has grown worse. I am planning to leave him. If you can't make the meeting I know you are busy and will understand.*
>
> *I am anxious to learn about your successes.*
>
> *All my love, Lea.*

Tomorrow would be good enough. Maybe he'd learn more about what was going on in the meantime. He'd have a chance to check out anything else he could learn about Rensler plus see how good his gift horse might be by riding him up there to her cabin. He could imagine her taking elegant steps across the room to him while wearing little clothing. Whew, he almost shuddered at the notion.

He ate supper in a larger restaurant and enjoyed a big steak. Halfway through his meal, a man slid into the chair opposite him, removed his hat, and shoved his hand over. He looked around to be certain no one was close enough to hear. "I'm Jake Helm. We met in Arizona a few years back."

Slocum nodded, recalling the burly man in the flannel shirt and suspenders. "What can I do for you?"

"What are you doing up here?"

"Looking for a killer. Why?"

"How can I help you?"

"I'm not certain. The man is on the run."

"Where do you think he's at?" Helm looked around the room, then turned back to Slocum. "You saved my life once. I want to help you."

"What are you doing up here?"

"Taking a herd of cattle to a beef contractor. We've been grazing five hundred head up here to deliver them to the beef contractor up at Douglas."

"Ward Provisions Company?" Slocum said, looking hard at him.

"Yeah, why?"

"This man I'm looking for is somehow connected to them and may be up there."

"Eat your meal." He shook his head at the waiter who came by to check on the new arrival. "How will I let you know what I find out up there?"

"Send word to Sam Houston at his livery here."

"All right. If he's up there I can find out in a few days. Who is he?"

"Ralph Rensler."

"I don't know him, but if he's up there, I'll get you word."

Slocum thanked him and stood up to shake his hand. At least he had some help. Things might not turn out as bad as he had envisioned. Tomorrow, he'd meet Lea and maybe in the next few days get some leads from some of his contacts. Good enough.

After supper he went and took a bath, had a shave, and got his hair cut. He left the barbershop and went back to the hotel. He'd see about his new horse in the morning.

After breakfast the next day he strode to the stables, and with Sam's man Eric, went out back and chose a stout roan horse. Eric handed him a lariat and Slocum slipped into the pen of a dozen horses. Whirling the loop over his head, he caught the roan, who put on the brakes. Glad that the roan knew enough to respect a lariat, he led him out and saddled him, all the time considering how hard the gelding could buck. With the horse rested and well fed, it would be a disappointment for him not to crow hop anyway.

"Will he buck?" he asked Eric.

"He damn sure might."

"I'll plan on it then," said Slocum, and they both laughed. When he bridled him, he looked at his teeth and considered him a four- or five-year-old.

"Guess we'll see how he acts." Eric laughed. "He might be a handful."

Taking the bridle cheek strap in his hand, Slocum used the stirrup to swing up into the saddle and let go of the bridle after he found the other stirrup. Roan danced around in the alleyway with him checking the anxious horse with the bit. At last he set spurs to him, and Roan ran to the other end without a buck, sliding to a halt. Coming back, Slocum nodded at the man. "He's quiet enough for me."

"Should make you a real good horse."

"I agree. Thank Sam for me. I'll be back."

"See ya." Eric waved and Slocum started for the north road. He soon headed up the west fork of what folks called the Bozeman Trail. With no notion of exactly where Lea's big house was at, he short loped Roan until he came to the turnoff on the map and rode west, then onto the two ruts headed toward the mountains. The country was rolling, and he wound around on the road. Checking the sun time, he figured he'd be early. He drew up on the rise and could see the small lake and the log cabin. No sign of anyone, but some dimples on the water surface told him some fish were feeding.

The sign read Private Property, No Trespassing or Fishing Allowed. He dismounted and opened the gate. With Roan inside, he closed it and rode on. He loosened the cinch, then left him saddled in the corral with water and hay inside a shelter. Then he went to the front porch and lay down in a hammock. The shade provided a cool enough place in the south wind. In minutes he was asleep.

At the sound of horses, he quickly awoke, raised his hat brim, and saw Lea driving two gaited horses pulling a surrey coming toward the house from the gate. She had arrived. He waited on the porch standing by the four-by-four milled post.

"Well," she said, smiling big as she pulled up at the end of the steep walk. "I see you found my hideout." Tying off the team, she rushed to him with her blue dress hem in her hand.

"Great place here," he said, taking her in his arms.

"It was his first place in Wyoming. There are some nice fish in the lake too."

She removed a set of keys from her dress pocket and unlocked the door. He swept her up in his arms—a move that startled her—and he carried her over the threshold. She squeezed his face and kissed him.

"You are a delightful man." •

Looking around, he spotted the large bed in the center of the room and let her down on it. She began chewing on her full lower lip. "Now?"

"Good as any."

"Damn right," she said and went to unlacing her shoes.

Once out of her footwear, she started to unbutton her dress. Pausing, she looked at him. "You doing the same?"

"No, I was enjoying watching you."

She never gave him any more chance to explain. She tackled him. They both fell back on the bed, laughing. Clothes, boots, everything went flying between kisses and fondling until they were naked. Then they turned to serious mouth to mouth on a flight to heady passion.

Coupling, he drove in her deep, and she clutched him with no reservations. Nothing held back, they fought for the peak. Again and again, until her internal muscles began to make spastic grasps at his plunger. Their tempo of excitement rose higher than the Rockies beyond the lake and cabin until he exploded deep inside her and she slipped off into a near faint. They simply lay there in each other's arms, done in and dazzled by the excitement of the chase.

"I have food in the surrey. Maybe we better put the horses up. How long can you stay?"

"No timetable on my part." He sat up and tried to clear his head. "What about you?"

"He won't be back for a week, maybe more. I don't really care for being bored all that time."

"You said you were going to leave him."

"I am, whenever he comes back. He doesn't need me and I don't need to live out here, cut off from my own world. I didn't find any country dances—"

"Did you look?"

"Not really. Trust me, I am not cut out for being the rancher's wife."

He lay back down, then turned on his side to look at her and tease her nearest nipple. She smiled. "You don't understand."

"I understand well. There's not enough activity to keep you here."

"Right, I am not your sit-at-home-and-knit little woman."

He reached over and pulled her closer to kiss. *Damn, what a woman.*

19

At dawn the next morning, Slocum used her husband's expensive fly rod and caught several nice cutthroat trout. With only an unbuttoned shirt on, he waded out to reach the fish and, whipping the weighted line out, he had another strike. The hook set, he began reeling in his fourth keeper.

Lea came down in a flannel gown. "Isn't that water cold?"

"Not bad when you're busy catching fish."

She laughed and hugged herself. "You want them fixed for breakfast?"

"I figured they'd be good enough."

"Ah, trout for breakfast coming up, but you must clean them for me."

"You've never done that?" he asked, backing out of the water to land his fish on the shore. He laughed. "I bet this is the most expensive rod and reel I've ever used too."

"No doubt. Nothing but the best for my husband."

"How's he going to take the news?"

"My leaving him? Badly. He does not like to lose."

"I don't blame him. I'd sure hate to lose you."

"Maybe if he'd excited me even one time I might stay.

But he never will. I am just another trophy, and each session, he is in such a hurry to simply have it over."

"Can't help you." Bent over, he used his sharp jackknife to cut the fishes' throats and make an incision from the anal port upward. Then, from the cut below the throat, he pulled guts and gills out. He proceeded to wash the first one out and then quickly repeated it on the others and laid them on the grass.

"Take their heads off, please. I don't want any eyes looking at me."

"Yes, ma'am." And he did it.

They quickly kissed, then he strung the fish on a small limb for her to carry. She thanked him and he wound up the line. Behind her, he came back up the hill. He'd seen four mule deer watering at the lake's edge earlier. Paradise of a place. Whew, she made the topping on the cake. He drew in the cool, piney smelling air—absolutely heaven.

Three days later they parted. She never mentioned not seeing him again. But he figured she didn't want to cross that bridge, and he rode the salty acting roan out the gate behind her. Then he dismounted to close it. She rushed back and kissed him.

"I wish I'd never met you. Your spear in my heart hurts me so."

"Likewise, you can be sure," he said and let her go.

The ride back Cheyenne seemed twice as long as his ride out there. When he dismounted at the livery, Sam rushed out with a message. "Where have you been? I've got two notes for you that say this guy Rensler is in Douglas."

"Good news. I better catch a train."

Sam looked at his pocket watch. "You can catch the nine-ten. We'll put your horse up. Ride him down to the depot and take your saddle with you. You may need it up there."

Slocum agreed as he read the two messages from his informants.

Rensler is staying in the Rosebud Hotel in Douglas and

gambling every day in the Crown Saloon. Need help, me and the boys will back you. Jake Helm.

Your man is in the Rosebud, room 212. My man says he gambles every day across the street. John Doolin.

Nice of them. Sam sent a boy along to bring back the roan horse. Slocum dismounted and unsaddled him at the depot and tipped the lad. Then he went inside and bought a northbound ticket for Douglas.

"You're plumb lucky. This ticket will get you all the way. They finished the tracks two days ago. You used to have to ride a mud wagon the last few miles to get there."

"Good," Slocum said, then went to sit on one of the pews in the lobby.

Ten hours or so away from his goal. He could hope that Rensler was still there. The man would not expect for anyone to find him, gambling across the street from the Rosebud Hotel. There should be no problem finding him, at any rate. Maybe the town law would help him. The federal warrant paid two hundred dollars for Rensler's capture. Most small town lawmen didn't make that much in six months. But the railroad being there might make the law high priced because all such boomtowns turned overnight into a circus of gunfighters, tinhorn gamblers, pickpockets, fugitives, and rowdy whores. He'd been there and seen the swift changes turn a town the way a blue northern could turn into a blizzard's blast in ten minutes.

During the night he slept on the bench seat by himself. Disturbed by the clack of the expansion joints, he drifted in and out of sleep. There was no way he could truly get any rest.

The sun came up the next day, and bleary-eyed, he got off at a train stopover and bought some hot coffee and Danishes. The coffee tasted like soap and the Danishes were three days old. A pleasant Dutch girl stopped him. "Sir, I've got some real pastry in my things on the train."

"Good," he said, and handed the rest of his purchases to a rumple-suited man who looked penniless. "Here, I have more."

"Huh, oh, thanks."

"Don't mention it," he said and followed the Dutch girl in the blue bonnet back on board the train.

She motioned for him to sit across from her. "My name is Greta. I am so glad to meet'cha."

"Mine's Slocum. Glad to meet you as well."

"I saw you eating those dried up things and I say to myself, 'I can help that cowboy. I've got much fresher things than he bought.' I am sorry you were out the money for them."

"No problem, but I appreciate your concern for me. Where are you going, Greta?"

She swallowed hard. "I am going to help my aunt in Douglas at her bakery."

"Where do you come from?"

"Oh, I was born in Holland, but I have been over here eighteen months."

"You speak English very well."

"Good, I want to become an American so much."

The pastry she fed him was apple something. And she was right: It and the cinnamon melted in his mouth. He wiped his mouth and thanked her. "And you should do very well in this business up here."

With a pleased smile, she nodded. "I hope so. What will you do up here?"

"Oh, I have some business to handle."

"Well, I shall hope it goes very well for you. Do you have a wife?"

"No, ma'am."

"I find that hard to believe."

"Well, that is the way it is."

"I am so sorry. I did not wish to pry."

"No problem. Tell me about Holland."

"Oh, it is a lovely country, but I love Wyoming."

"Good, many women can't stand it." He thought of Lea and her distress with the country.

Their conversation went on for miles. Greta proved to be a very darling young woman, and he had no doubts she would soon find herself a man of her own in the wilds of this land.

Then they arrived in Douglas and the conductor said, "All off."

He leaned over and kissed his Dutch companion on the cheek. "You will blow them over up here." Shocked, she held the tips of her fingers to the place on her cheek like it was a burning spot.

"I'm sorry. I had to kiss you for being so nice to me."

"Oh, it was nothing."

He rose to get off the train. "And have fun becoming an American. We need more people like you."

The saddle on his shoulder, he left the train. Douglas was a sleepy little town on a large river for the west, the North Platte. The place would soon bustle with the railroad's arrival. He decided to walk the few blocks to the two-story building marked Rosebud Hotel.

"Have any rooms?" he asked the clerk and then swung down his saddle.

Definitely not a plush place, he waited as the man searched his register. "Oh, yes, I have one. Second floor back."

"How much?"

"Seven-fifty."

"That is outrageous," he said to the man.

"It is what we get for a room. We only have one to rent."

Slocum dug the money out of his pocket and paid the clerk for two nights. No telling how long this would take. After his night ride on the train with so little sleep, he decided to take a few hours' shut-eye. He'd need all his wits about him to take on Rensler. The man might even have some of his associates with him.

He awoke later than he had planned, washed his face in the bowl, brushed his hair down, and then checked the chambers of his .45. With it holstered, he was ready. He went downstairs and crossed the street to the Crown Saloon. Not over half full, still the room was hazed in tobacco smoke. He stepped to the bar and ordered a beer. The mustached man brought him back one for a dime. That price would soon soar as well.

Then he saw a familiar hat on the back of a man's head. The man who sat across the room at the card game was Ralph Rensler. So busy playing cards he hadn't noticed Slocum's arrival.

Slocum watched his man having a sharp-spoken argument with another player. Everyone saw the situation was getting out of hand, and they fled the table. One player who tried to get up turned over his chair. In haste, he crawled away on the nasty sawdust floor. The two men faced each other across the table.

Slocum knew it was only a moment or two until Rensler saw him as well. He drew his own weapon. "Both of you men raise your hands. Now!"

Rensler's eyes flew open, but he could see the gun ready in Slocum's hand. He shoved his own hands higher. The other man turned with his arms in the air and blinked at Slocum's gun.

"This man is wanted for the murder of two of my employees in the Indian Territory. Stand aside," he told the other man.

"All right, marshal," the other man agreed. "But he's a lying cheat."

"I can't help that. Rensler, walk this way. One misstep and you're dead."

"You can't arrest me. You're no marshal."

"You can die in your boots. I think I'd like that." Everyone was parted so his shot would be clear. "Now you decide."

"Don't shoot. But you can't hold me."

"We'll see. Judge Parker won't extend you any bond."

"I've got lawyers—"

He was close enough that Slocum reached for Rensler's handgun in his holster. He saw Rensler move and he slammed him over the head with the barrel of his gun. The blow drove Rensler to his knees and he cried out. Slocum managed to disarm him and step back. But Rensler's jerk and subsequent other moves caused an ace of spades to flutter from his sleeve and show faceup on the floor.

"Lynch the cheating sumbitch!" someone shouted.

An angry roar from the crowd went up and Slocum, who'd holstered his own six-gun, found himself being restrained against the bar by several men. Nothing he could do. Rensler was dragged out the batwing doors screaming, but the rush of men was not to be put aside.

"You going to interfere?" one bearded man who was well over six and a half feet tall demanded of Slocum, pressing him against the bar.

Slocum shook his head at his captors. The three agreed and left. They rushed out the doors to catch the lynch mob.

"You want another beer on the house?" the bartender asked from behind him.

"No." Slocum shook his head as his efforts drained from him. "Make it a double of good whiskey."

"Coming up. That was some deal. Did you believe it was going to happen like that?"

Slocum wet his lips and considered the liquor in the glass on the bar. Damn, what a day. "No, I didn't."

"Where are you headed next?"

"I'm not certain." Slocum tossed down the smooth booze and looked around the empty room. Unusual for him not to have a destination. "Maybe I'll go find some Dutch pastry."

The barkeep frowned and then shook his head, like his words made no sense. "You want more whiskey?"

"No, thanks." He pushed the Colt down in his holster and started on his way out the double doors. Under the porch roof, out of the sun's glare, he looked hard at the strangling figure dancing on the end of the rope. No slow death for Rensler, but he wouldn't struggle for long. The man responsible for Bronc and Wolf's death had met his fate on the end of a rope.

He walked two blocks and found the pastry shop. Wonderful smells of things being baked filled the air. The bell rang overhead in the entrance as he stepped inside.

He removed his hat and smiled at the straight-backed woman with her gray hair in a bun. "Good day. Is Greta here?"

"Oh, yes, she is."

Greta came out in a starched white apron. "Oh, how are you? This is my aunt."

"Nice to meet you. Would you have supper with me this evening?"

"Oh, I don't know. We may have more things to bake."

"Greta, for goodness' sake, this nice man wants to buy your supper. Of course she will. What time?"

"Six o'clock be all right?"

"Yes," her aunt said. "She will be ready."

He touched his hat and looked hard at Greta. "That is all right?"

"Oh, yes. I will be ready. Thank you." She curtsied for him.

"What was all that shouting and yelling about a few minutes ago?" Greta's aunt asked.

"Oh, they simply hung a man caught cheating at cards."

"Wyoming is a very hard place," she said.

"No, ma'am, it handles its own problems. See you at six." Then he started to leave.

"Wait, I want you to taste our pastry," Greta said as if recovered from her silence.

Her aunt agreed and he left their shop carrying a paper sack of pastries and chewing on a cherry-covered sweet roll. It did taste wonderful. To match his sunny Wyoming day.

Watch for

SLOCUM ALONG CORPSE RIVER

391st novel in the exciting SLOCUM series
from Jove

Coming in September!